# VAMPIRES OF CAMELOT

## DESMORIA'S DOWNFALL

### PART III

*Thank you for your support. I hope you enjoy it*

*Joanne Padgett*

*More Praises for Joanne Padgett*
*Vampires of Camelot*
*Desmoria's Downfall*
*Part III*

" My favorite kind of book is the sort that takes to the edge of your seat from start to finish Vampires of Camelot is one of those stories that let's your breath the air of another time I can think of no better adventure." *Dianna Reid*

"The author builds a powerful adventure story animating everyone- Merlin, Solana, Uther Pendragon, The animals of war alike in a gorgeous vividly described landscapes the erotic passages are riveting!"

*- Booklist*

"The captivating epic novel series Vampires of Camelot in hands down a new take on the Camelot story that will leave the readers wanting more."

*- Examiner*

"Joanne Padgett is a skilled story teller who easily weaves historical fact with romantic ambience to create a complex design ….. Exemplary historical thriller that will keep you on the edge of your seat." *-Mt Juliet News*

# VAMPIRES OF CAMELOT

# DESMORIA'S DOWNFALL PART III

All rights reserved Copyright© 2015 by Joanne Padgett
Cover Art designed by Joel Robinson © VOC Entertainment Inc.
Library of Congress catalog number 97-54853
No part of this book may be reproduced or transmitted without written authorization from the author
ISBN-13: 978-1515374947

Dedication Page

For my Fang Buddies first and foremost I am honored to have all of you in my life I want to thank my family and friends for all their help and support of this wonderful dream that started in 2009.

For Chloe, Ash, Tiffany, and Jason live your dreams and make them a reality.

For my dearest heart Gerald always and forever to the moon and back

Thank you to Stephanie my editor who helped make this project great

Richard & Betty Joe our bloodlines are forever entwined together thank you for embracing my writing and always giving me encouragement

# VAMPIRES OF CAMELOT
# DESMORIA'S DOWNFALL

## TABLE OF CONTENTS

| | |
|---|---|
| PREFACE | 06 |
| MERLIN'S REBIRTH | 21 |
| JEWELS OF TIME | 28 |
| INGRIEN'S DISGRACE | 35 |
| SOLANA'S STRATAGEM | 61 |
| DESMORIA'S SCHEME | 81 |
| MERLIN'S ASSAULT | 91 |
| GAWAIN'S ARMY | 111 |
| THE SEARCH FOR UTHER | 125 |
| THE MANICORE RELEASE | 142 |
| THE TOMB OF THE ANIMALS OF WAR | 167 |
| THE LOVE STONE | 177 |
| LUCIFER'S BLUEPRINT | 186 |
| SOLANA RETRIEVES THE MOON STONE | 200 |
| THE STAFF OF POWER | 217 |
| TARNISH IS A VAMPIRE | 224 |
| DESMORIA'S DOWNFALL | 231 |

# PREFACE

Uther is under Helena's control as she seeks justice for the death of her people. Helena begins to free the animals of war to kill the Minotaur and end the reign of the gods forever. Merlin is trapped in another time with Desmoria who has taken on the life of Ezerbeth Bathory to inflict horror upon the world and bring forth the true depths of hell on Earth.

Garlois, Gawain, and Tarnish must find a way to rule the lands in harmony. Gawain and Tarnish are building their forces to protect their lands. Garlois must find out why Ingrien's father stopped the knights training. Garlois as king must try to produce an heir so that the kingdom will flourish.

Ingrien struggles with life as a queen. She wanted nothing out of life but to be a healer and now she is queen of the lands by the sea. Ingrien still lusts for Uther and Garlois is pressuring her to conceive so that the kingdom will continue.

Solana is a brink of despair for she has lost Merlin. She wanted to denounce the goddess and not be The Lady of the Lake. The goddess was angered by this and told Solana that was not her choice. She is a vessel of the goddess now and forever.

Merlin has lost his mind. He does not know who he is or why he is here. Merlin knows deep within himself that something is not right. Merlin and Frédéric go and search for answers.

Merlin is caught up in a whirl wind of confusion he knows there is something desperately wrong. Frédéric also senses something amiss in the presences of Merlin. He knows that no person should be able to heal that quickly from the wounds he suffered. Frédéric tries to rationalize it by saying it was the will of god but still he has never seen a miracle quite like Merlin. "Frédéric I know we're close I can feel it" Merlin is filled with a surge of power. His body seems to be growing with voltage building this heat pulsating through his whole being when he reaches the spot of his accident as the voltage fills his body he sees flashes of lights in all colors surrounding his thoughts vibrate blues hues of purple in circle patterns fill his head.

Merlin's graze on his head starts to glow and iridescent bluish yellow as his wound becomes a bright green. Merlin glances in the distance and spots a beautiful woman but she is cascaded in another image. Underneath is a vision of beauty he has never seen. Her eyes two dark pools of magnificent black beauty. She has silky white skin, slim features, ripe plentiful breasts, and strong long legs that round into the perfect backside.

Merlin is bewitched by this creature he reaches out his hands to touch this divine creature and as he does the woman fades away in the distance. Merlin is perplexed as he scans for the beautiful creature he spots the sands of time as they start to unravel opening a portal. Merlin watches the vision of beauty as she goes into the portal and he caught sight of himself following her into the portal then everything fades to black. Merlin faints dead away in Freidrick's arms.

Ezerbeth Bathoray was a stunningly beautiful with her fair alabaster skin her long luscious brown silken hair. She had a small petite frame with supple curves that accentuates her. Desmoria was lucky to take over such a beautiful creature. She knew that Merlin followed her in the time stream but she had no idea where he was.

Desmoria was running out of time and knew she had to work fast to make sure that she met her agreement with Lucifer. As Ezerbeth she must maintain her nobility Desmoria/Ezerbeth knew she must have an heir to take over the throne. She knew that she was the creature of magic. Desmoria contemplated, "*How can I maintain this rouse? How can I have a child? How will I maintain my strength? I do not want to bring attention to myself but I am ravenous for blood.*"
As Desmoria/Ezerbeth was thinking she was struck with genius on how to maintain her rouse and build up her blood supply as well as having a child.

She would venture out in secret to gathering peasant females from across the lands who were of birth giving age. She would lure these women with broken promises of becoming a lady of the court. Once the girls accepted they were whisked off to the castle where she would imprison them. Desmoria/Ezerbeth would use a spell of glamor to masquerade them as mirror images of herself. She would then place them under a trance controlling the women.

Desmoria/Ezerabeth would have them lay with her husband. The women would give birth to heirs for the throne and not cause any dissention within the court.

She scoured the countryside and choose several peasants to give birth to children. Demoria/Ezerbeth used the purple stone amulet to cast a spells on the peasant girls. She knew using the amulet would deplete her powers but it was the only way to conceal the peasant girls to lay with her husband in Ezerbeth's form.

Desmoria/Ezerbeth began with the first peasant girl she noticed her from the street. The girl was frail she looked to be about twenty years old. The girl sat on the side of the street begging for food. She told the carriage driver to approach the girl. As she locked eyes with the innocent girl she looked deep within her soul penetrating blue eyes. The girl grew unnerved as if frighten by the Lady Ezerbeth.

Desmoria/Erzabeth placed the young girl in a trance as she whispered. "Do not be sadden little one I will take all your pain away." Desmoria/Ezerbeth knew she needed to feed but she must only take what was needed for this would be the first of her sex slaves to give birth. The girl was transfixed in a mesmerizing state. Desmoria/Ezerbeth held out her hand and grabbed the girl. **All I need is a little taste,** she thought.

Her appetite was massive she longed for blood as the rhythmic pulse of the girls heart sent her into a frenzy. The fangs began to leap from her mouth as she sunk her teeth deep within the girl's chest.
Desmoria/Ezerbeth drank the life source from her heart until the girl was knocked insensible. She took her back to the castle once there she transformed the girl into Lady Ezerbeth using a glamorous spell. Desmoria/Ezerbeth held her magi amulet as she recited, "Wood and Wind, Ember and Mist Grant your blessed child's wish
Sacred goddess charge this amulet
Let you power and light make this wretched peasant divine exchange our outer selves
Hers and mine wrap us in your sweet glow
So that each of us becomes the other tis all that anyone will see and know."

Desmoria's/ Ezerbeth's violet pendent started to light up Beams of light surrounded the two of them as the metamorphosis came over both of them as their outer selves changed the small meek peasant girl was changed into Ezerbeth's image and Desmoria was changed into the peasant girl.

The peasant girl fainted in the transformation Desmoria took the girl up to Ferenc bed chamber.
The girl was frazzled and unaware of where she was when she came too. The girl was in the royal bed chamber. The girl noticed a glimpse of herself in the mirror horror filled her face. "This

cannot be? How did this happen?" Before she could utter another word the Count entered the room. He was sadist sort who loved to torture. A devilish smile broad across his face as Ferenc approached the bed and the girl lay in wait unaware of what to do. "I see you are ready with anticipation for our tryst good lady. I love to see the fear in your eyes but wait the best is yet to come!!!" He replied excitedly.

The girl froze with utter terror unable to move. Ferenc hurried to disrobe to unveil his engorged throbbing manhood. It was a long hard shaft wrapped in a tight twine to hold his erection.
The girl's hands were bound to the bed with thorn branches of wicker when she moved her wrist surged with the pain as the blood trickled down her arms.

He moved closer watching her thrash about. He circled the bed growing more and more excited at her anguish as Ferenc reached the amour where the tools of torture were hidden.

He grabbed the claw which was a long whip of fine Corinthian leather attached to a silver hand like claw. Ferenc eyes widen with pleasure, "I believe this will be the ecstasy of the night my dear" Ferenc took the whip and started to slash and cut the wife/peasant girl she let out a howling scream. "Yes that's it more you know I need more scream for me." He cut and slashed her as her garment was torn to shreds to reveal a tight corset underneath. Ferenc grabbed another love tool from the amour this was a jeweled knife.

Ferenc approached the bed to a sobbing fearful girl. His lust for her was overwhelming he reached for her. The girl was tied to the bed blood covered her body from the cuts and scrapes. Ferenc engorged with lust began to feel the girl shake frighten in his strong arms as he took his hands and rubbed and squeezed her ripe bloody nipples hurting and tearing at her flesh.

Licking the blood from her wounds and taking the knife and teasing her. The cold steel of the knife against her skin her body quivered and shook with fear knowing he would stab her at any moment. The girl fainted dead away.

Ferenc had reached his ultimate high as he took the knife and cut her corset off. "Yes the lady has given me pleasure I will take her now." Forcing himself into her over and over in a vigorous motion hard and fast as she lay lifeless.

"Yes Ezerbeth I am lord and master I will take what is mine. I will give my devil seed to flourish within you. Ferenc released and lay with the lifeless girl as the blood coursed through her onto the bed he knew his bride was a virgin no more. Desmoria/Ezerbeth waited until the deed was done watching with delight at Ferenc and his ability to torture.

Desmoria/Ezerbeth slipped in when he was fast asleep and took the peasant girl down to the cellar. She chained the peasant to the wall and waited. Desmoria/Ezerbeth did this several times to make sure a child was conceived. If a child was not conceived then she would take the girls and drain them of their blood. If a child was conceived she would take the peasant girl feed and clothe her in the dungeon until the peasant gave birth and in that moment when the child was born a servants would come and take the child away.

Desmoria/Ezerbeth would creep into the cellar afterward she would console the peasant girl. She would embrace and caress them in her arms. Leading the peasant girl in a false sense of security. Desmoria/Ezerbeth would then take her knifelike fingernails and rake then across the throat of the peasant girl instantly ripped out her throat.
She would then hoist the peasant girl upside down where a barrel would collect every ounce of scarlet fluid. She would then take vials of blood from the barrel until it was emptied as the peasant girl lay lifeless Desmoria/Ezerbeth ate the afterbirth of each child. After which she have the peasant girl taken and thrown away into the gutter like a piece of lowly trash.
Desmoria/Ezerbeth would send the children away.

Now it seems as time is coming ever closer and she is doomed to repeat the same mistakes. Desmoria/Ezerbeth was about to continue her ritual when she was struck down by a bolt of lightning. For the first time in her life she had felt fear as she looked upon Merlin.

Desmoira/Ezerbeth was taken distressed as she look at image of Merlin he had aged and was more powerful than before. Merlin's young blond hair had turned white his soft skin was now wrinkled and worn. Merlin was mesmerized by the sight of Desmoria/Ezerbeth. The sands of time surrounded them both opening the portal as she relived the journey. She saw how Merlin had fallen and ended up in Vienna. Desmoria/Ezerbeth watched the vision as she saw that Merlin had sustained injury to the head. She knew it was time to act time to bring Merlin to the dark side before he regained his memory of her.

She made haste to Vienna hoping that she would be in time to change Merlin to corrupt him to dark magic. Desmoria/Ezerbeth knew then she will be able to pay her debt to Lucifer and she will be free to rule the world and exact her revenge on Man.

Pegasus was at last freed from his prison. He knelt his head down toward Helena and she placed the bridle in his mouth.

Once the bridle was in his mouth flashes of light veered into his head as he witnessed his imprisonment into his prison. He saw the god's capture him and the other animals of war. He witnessed where the other animals were being held. Pegasus reared up and screamed out in horror as he caught sight of the goddess.
"It was her the goddess she had returned. I still don't believe my eyes my dear sweet friend how could the Gods do this? How could they turn on their own creations like that? It was the Goddess she turned the gods against us. It was her that led the attack upon us.

I remember now she took all of the animals of war and scattered them to the four winds. She had entomb me within the Earth because I had power over the skies. She trapped the phoenix within the sea because of its power of fire. The leviathan is held on the top of Mount Olympus to look down toward the sea and never be able to feel his true world.

But the last dear animal of war was entombed in the rock of ages there it was held in time and space never to walk among the fields the great Manicore.
The horror of it all is beyond me. I am truly filled with sorrow and pain for what has been done. Helena who is this Uther that freed me why is he on my mane."

Pegasus shook his head and Uther was thrown down to the ground. As he was thrown Excalibur landed on the ground and Pegasus fell to the ground under Excalibur's power. "What Magic is this that the mortal wields that hold such power over me?"

"It is Excalibur great Pegasus the sword of the Hyperion age made from ancient steel and forged by the hands of the gods." Helena replied. Uther stood on his feet and took Excalibur from the ground and held it in his hand. Pegasus was overcome with rage he took to the heavens as he leapt into the air the great force shook the ground as thunder claps were heard for miles.

Helena shouted "Pegasus come back, we must free the others and put an end to the god's tyranny forever."

Pegasus flew high above the clouds and soared in the air. He was a sight to behold the majestic creature flying in the air like a bird. Helena ordered Uther to throw Excalibur in the air as hard as he could. Uther under her control took the mighty sword and threw it up in the air towards Pegasus.

The sword of power began to glow a dazzling green and lit up the sky forcing Pegasus to the ground. Pegasus crash landed near the field as he gained his footing he stood stunned for a few moments just enough time for Helena to latch her hands onto the bridle and with one swift motion she pulled Pegasus back to Uther.

Uther watch as Excalibur was in the air and his eyes grew with astonishment when he set his eyes on the vibrant emerald color that engulfed the sky forcing Pegasus to the ground. **"By the gods the power from Excalibur grows stronger the more I use it what magic is this and how can I control it?"** Uther thought to himself as Helena raced to capture Pegasus. Helena with Pegasus in hand was growing evermore annoyed with his flights of fancy agitated, "We do not have time for this nonsense Pegasus we need to free the other animals of war and we must act quickly before it is known that I have freed you."

"Helena I have been locked away from this world for centuries and I see much has changed but still some things remain the same. I to want to seek my vengeance on the gods for what they have done. I am not accustom to being a part of a team effort I usually work alone."

Helena was enraged as she shouted, "You do not have the pleasure of working alone we need Uther to free the other animals of war Pegasus!"

   Solana was on a verge of madness she felt utter despair for years she search for Merlin unable to find her true love. Solana wanted to walk away from the goddess and Avalon forever but she was chained to her duties as vessel to the goddess.

Solana every attempt to walk away was extinguished by the goddess. Solana knew her only refuge was to go along until she could find a way to grow her powers and seek her freedom. Solana knew the only way to that was to lay in wait when the goddess is vulnerable and then exact her retribution.

Solana studied the charts of magic and learned of still one more way to find Merlin.
Solana had to find the crystal of light hidden deep with the Earth. The crystal of light would show her the path of Merlin. Only then could she use her power of the love bond to summon him back. Solana could not leave the confines of Avalon. Solana must seek outside help to get the crystal of light and finally reunite with Merlin. Gawain was hard at work training his forces and leading his kingdom. He knew that the best defense was to have an arsenal cable of anything. Gawain knew the horror left in the past with the vampires and he would not let any such creature damn him or his kingdom. Gawain had to choose the best men in the land and start their knights training.

Gawain was taught as a mere boy when he started his knight training. He did not have the benefit now, however; most of the men were grown in the kingdom and he had to teach then the fundamentals of knight training. Gawain started all the men at squire level. Each of the men were given different tasks to master depending on their strength and capabilities. The knighthood training consisted of acquiring excellent equestrian skills.

A horse played an extremely important part in the life of a knight. A knight would own several horses which were built for different duties. These knights ranged in various sizes starting with a palfrey, or an ambler for general traveling purposes. Bigger and stronger horses were required as warhorses.

The Courser was the most sought after and expensive warhorse, owned by the wealthiest knights. The more common warhorses were like modern hunters, known then as destroyers.

The apprentice knights would learn how to ride and control their horses and the art of this type of warfare. Starting with small ponies they would hone their equestrian skills in their knighthood training.

The squires were also expected to play their part of caring for the horses in the stables.

Gawain squires ranged from fourteen to twenty-one. Most of the squires learned the basic skills required during their childhood training. As Squires they were seen as men capable of fighting in battles. Their knighthood training became far more dangerous. Injuries were a common occurrence during their knighthood training. Their skills with the lance had to be perfected. The tool used in the practice of the lance was called the quatrain.

The quatrain consisted of a shield and dummy which was suspended from a swinging pole. When the shield was hit by a charging squire, the whole apparatus would rotate. The squire's task was to avoid the rotating arms and not get knocked from his saddle.
A variation of the quatrain added heavy swinging sandbags which also had to be avoided. Accuracy was also an important factor and squires practiced "Running at the Rings" where the lance was aimed at a target in the shape of a ring - these rings were obviously much smaller to lance than a man and this skill was therefore difficult to master.

Fighting with quarterstaffs could also result in injuries. Fighting with swords and other weapons were strictly supervised and only wooden, blunt or covered weapons were used. General fitness levels had to be high and the strength of an apprentice knight was expected, regardless of size.

Gawain had built a fighting force in his squires and know they must prove their worth. Gawain beckoned the squires to gather together. All the squires gathered in the meeting hall.

"I have watched all of you and I believe you have mastered the skills to be knights. It is time that you take the oath. You squires of the realm do hereby pledge your lives for your king to protect the kingdom at all costs. You squires will invoke the rights of chivalry and valor to defend the innocent. What say you squires?"

The squires look to one another and in unison answer granted dear king Gawain we so do pledge ourselves as knight to defend and uphold the honor of the kingdom.

"Come fourth and accept your knighthood men." With that each of the men approached the king and Gawain dubbed them knights. A feast was prepared to celebrate the knights of the realm as they danced and feasted into the night.

Gawain sat at the head as king and the first time it hit him he would be ruler of all he surveyed he carried the weight of these men and their lively hood. Gawain knew it was time to act and to move forward with is goal to occupy more lands and to exact money for the treasury from the people now that he has his elite fighting force of warriors

# CHAPTER ONE
# MERLIN'S REBIRTH

Merlin was overtaken and fainted dead away in Frédéric's arms. Merlin wound was still glowing his forehead became burning hot. Frédéric tried to revive Merlin using herbs to jolt his senses. Merlin could smell the horrible aroma of sulfur. The pungent smell of soiled eggs revived him.

Merlin's eyes flashed open and he rose to his feet.
"Frédéric you would not believe it I saw what happened. I saw the sands of time itself. It was marvelous the colors of vibrate purple the hues of blue and green.

I caught a glimpse of myself traveling through the whirlpool of time. I saw the most beautiful woman she was a vixen of pure delight. I ran after her through the whirlpool of time. Frédéric what could this mean?"
Frédéric listened in awe of what Merlin was saying. His eyes grew enlarged as Merlin continued with his story. Frédéric heard these words and was terrified. Frédéric was speechless. He looked to Merlin frightened and spoke with a timid whisper, "I do not know Merlin this is out of my depth. I fear the unknown it is not for us to say the will of the gods the way you speak it is as if you are a god yourself to travel through the sands of time is impossible.

Merlin looked to Frédéric with astonishment at his words, "How dare you suggest that I am god Freidrick! I am a man same as you I am mortal." As Merlin began to continue his mind's eye opened and he was shown his true destiny. Merlin was given a vision as the sparks in his head began to fire flashes of orange and yellow then as he dwell deeper the flashes of light changed into a crescent white tot a center of his mind once there Merlin started to remember.
Frédéric looked on to Merlin who was in a daze. Frédéric unaware of what to do grew more afraid and ran for his life. Merlin stood motionless as he journeyed deeper into his mind. Merlin recalled back to life on Koldacot his family Althea, Grandmissio, Ursula, Mab, and Norwick .

He looked on and saw the horrible fates that befell his parents at the hands of his twin sister Mab. He witnessed as Ursula was taken ill due to Mab and her selfish attempts to kill her family and be all powerful. Merlin watched Solana at Avalon as he feed from her bosom and almost killed his one true love.

Merlin was filled with memories of death and sorrow. He was filled with love and understanding. As he continued to watch his destiny unfold before his very eyes. Merlin saw how his twin sister Mab had succumb to death. Mab had become pregnant with the devil's spawn Desmoria. She was reborn on Earth. Mab was vanquished as she lie dying Desmoria wasted little time and feed from her own mother.
As she sank her fangs deep within her mother and drank of her until her life-force was gone. Desmoria was covered in black

blood of her mother as she walked unto the Earth once more. The horror of the site was more than Merlin could bear but still he pressed on after all he needed to know: *Why he was here? What prompted him to follow this women through the sands of time?*
Onward through the battle Merlin witnessed all of the agony once more as he saw so many die before his eyes the replication were far greater in number as they took innocent victims left and right. Merlin saw how he used his powers to end the suffering and killed all the replicants.
 He witnessed as Desmoria and Gallian were at each other and how Desmoria killed Gallian. He continued to look deeper to see the final horror as he watched Norwick's death at the hands of Desmoria. His body filled with rage as he hunted her. Merlin followed her to the depths and jumped into the sands of time.

Merlin knew why he had come here. Merlin wanted to kill Desmoria for her treachery. He wanted to end her once and for all. Merlin knew his task and knew he had to find Desmoria before it was too late and she began her desecration of this world. Merlin was shot straight up like a bolt of lightning out of his vision. Merlin looked for Frédéric as he scoured the landscape he was nowhere in sight. Merlin knew what he must do. Merlin had to find Desmoria. He needed to end her pitiful existence and he need to act quickly.
He had grown weak and needed to feed. Merlin knew he needed the magi blood to re-energize himself but he was in a foreign land and was unsure of how to proceed. He knew he needed to act there was no time for anything else. Merlin only knew of one

place that he would be able to obtain magi blood that was in Avalon.
There was little time to waste so with his last bit of energy Merlin used a transportation spell and he was instantly at Avalon. Merlin was standing on the shores of Avalon but what he saw was astonishing, the land was dark once the great city lay in ruble and ruin. The majestic cliff of Avalon lay in waste. Merlin looked in the cliff-face to see the once beautiful ivory castle was no more instead lay destruction and decay gone forever Avalon beloved Avalon. The goddess and all her alters were laid to waste. Merlin saw this dark desolate place in its wake.
"I am running on empty I have nowhere else to look I call to you goddess come to my aid." The ground beneath Merlin's feet began to quake air shot out of geysers and fishers within the structure of Avalon as the goddess appeared. "By the heavens is it really you? Merlin what has happened to you? I had forsaken this place long ago when the lady of lake turned her back on me."
Merlin was unable to utter a word for his strength was depleted. "Merlin speak to me Merlin!" The goddess shouted. Merlin could wait no longer hunger had taken over. Merlin fangs engorged and protruded out of his mouth as he sank his teeth within the goddess.
He drank of her filling himself. "Merlin stop!" Merlin you must not Merlin please stop!" Merlin could not hear her cries. Merlin feed upon her life-force he drank to fill his hunger he drank to refill his strength. The goddess concentrated all her energy and focused it all toward the center of Merlin's mouth. "Enough" she shouted and a powerful fireball exploded in Merlin's mouth forcing him to stop. Merlin's eyes were enlarged and the color

was a white gray as his fangs went back. His mind was clear and he was ashamed of what he had done. Merlin's heart was broken when he saw how Avalon had changed.
He looked to the goddess with shock and awe as he caught of sight of what he had done to her. Merlin ran to her said, "I am sorry I was overcome with hunger I could not control it goddess I am sorry."
"Merlin you do not know what you have done I am a goddess. Merlin the gods will now take vengeance upon you for what you have done by drinking my blood you have angered them and they will seek you out and destroy you."
Merlin did not care for her threats he only wanted to know what happened to Avalon. "Goddess what has happened to your temple? Where is Solana? What has happened to her?" Merlin you are in another time Solana is dead and gone she is not immortal. She is the lady of lake and under your protection why did you let her die. I did not let her die she choose her own path after you followed Desmoria into the future Solana was heartbroken and she had forsaken me. She vowed she would find a way to bring you back. Solana denounced me and Avalon in search of her heart and love for you.
Merlin the once a bright wonderful way of life have ended. The mortals stopped believing in the gods. They all were swept away by this savior, the one true God. It is unspeakable how they have forsaken us for this modern religion. They no longer believe in the Magi or dragons anymore. They are much more content with the church.
They cast out any that do not believe the way they do many wars have been fought in the name of the one true God Jehovah many

of my followers were killed in the war of the one mighty God. Why did you not intervene goddess? Why did you allow your followers to die horrible deaths? What has happened to this world? What has happened to mortals that they turn their backs on the gods? I know you have powers to end this threat and show mortals your true power goddess.
Merlin when mortals stopped believing in us we lose our powers. Not to mention the bitch Helena as she set to usurp all the gods in retaliation for her people. She took it upon herself to free the animals of war and plagues were set upon the Earth. War was fought between the gods and man and there were many causality. Zeus sent the horrible Titians on the world when his beloved Hera was struck down by Pegasus. He sent down massive thunderbolts and lay a path of destruction that left death only. The Manicore lay waste to griffin as he feed on the bones of mortal and gods alike. Uther Pendragon was under the spell of Helena aided her as he released the worst of animals of war the phoenix who set mount Olympus on fire killing all that was there. I have lied wait for you to return. Merlin I want to bring back the time of Avalon and stop Helena from her plan to destroy the gods.
Merlin looked deep within the goddess eyes with rage as he shouted, "I am not your pawn goddess I will not help you in this cause what has happened was meant to happened and I will not change it. I am here to put an end to Desmoria. She killed the only family I had left on this world. I am not interested in your plans. Once I find Desmoria and put end to her once and for all I will banish her to hellfire and watch as she burns for eternity. Then I will seek the help of Corons to return me to my time. I

will live out my days with Solana in Avalon and that will be the end of it. I will let the mortals do as they will for it does not affect me in the slightest."

 The goddess was now overcome with rage and frustration as she roared "Merlin everything that the mortals do will affect you and the course of time itself. If Helena goes through with her plans the world will be lost the gods will be lost so Cronos will not be able to bring you back through time don't you see we must go back now before it is too late. We must stop Helena from releasing the animals of war."

"You expect me to travel back to stop Helena why is she wanting to destroy the gods what happened to her people the tree creatures goddess that she would go to these lengths?" The goddess looked to Merlin with guilt in her eyes and spoke in a humble timid voice "That is not the point Merlin the point is if the events of the past continue it will be the end of time as we know it. It will be the end of Avalon and all you hold dear to your heart. You must come with me know there is no time to argue the point any longer. "Merlin looked at the goddess and cried out "What did you do I know Helena she wouldn't seek retaliation for no reason!!!!"

"Merlin you do not understand there are consequences for actions. Helena had no right to take the Hyde prisoner she had no right to trap my beloved Hyde. She had to be punished it was the only way I would not lose face with the people. I do not have to explain myself to you Merlin. Now come with me back to Avalon the time has come we have no more time to discuss this."

# CHAPTER TWO
# THE JEWELS OF TIME

Solana was overcome with heartache for Merlin. Her every thought was consumed by memories of her beloved. Avalon had lost its luster nothing could rival her affection for Merlin. She knew that there must be some way to bring him back. She studied all the scrolls looking for some way to bring him back.
Solana knew that without Merlin the world was going to die. Riddled with despair and heartache she looked to the goddess for help. Solana called out to the goddess to come to her aid. The goddess did not answer her call it was trivial to worry for love there was no reason to ache for a man. Solana is in a brink of despair for she has lost Merlin. She wanted to denounce the goddess and not be The Lady of the Lake. The goddess sensed Solana was troubled. The goddess knew her only option was to confront this and to make The Lady of Lake understood her place in the world. Solana had aged so much in the few months that Merlin had disappeared. She stopped caring about her appearance at all her lustrous beauty seemed to fade into the distance. Solana walked the walls of Avalon looking for any signs of happiness looking to the wall of history only brought her torment as she looked at the pictures of Merlin and magi tears would roll down her face as she sob in agony for Merlin.
The goddess appear from thin air as Solana wept uncontrollable.
"Solana what troubles you so that you are so cheerless?"
I.... I ...cannot cope I have lost Merlin I....I..... Unable to gain her composure Solana blurted out I'm nothing without him. Goddess

please I know it is within your power to find him. Goddess I must know where Merlin is don't you see how without out him the land is dying how the realm is changing."

The goddess was becoming enraged and shouted, "Solana get a hold of yourself you are The Lady of the Lake. Solana you should not let a man have so much power of over you!!"
In between sobs Solana bellowed, "You are god how could you even begin to know what I am feeling. Merlin is a part of me he is the half that makes me whole. Without out him I feel like I am empty.
Merlin is more than a mere man he is a part of this world. The goddess was stunned to hear Solana speak to her in such a manner that rage consuming her she screamed, "You speak of him as if he was God. Merlin is only flesh and bone he is mortal that is all he does not control the land or this realm. It is the will of the Gods that this famine is happening to teach the mortals the power of the Gods.
Mortals who have turned their backs on us for this new God the one true God Jehovah, son of God spouting about a sole and the heavens where all are equal and everything is blissful. The son who raised from the dead and walk upon the earth and Hades to free the tortured soles. Mortals and their fantasies who made a hero out of a meager mortal. He was not divine as the gods are he was just another plain mortal with no more power than you. Just as you hold Merlin on a pestle as your one true love he is no more than a man and as such he will disappoint you."
Solana listen to this goddess as she continued to speak of and the one true god. She listened as the goddess befouled her love for

Merlin and told her she was fool to let a man have so much power over her.

Solana thought about what the goddess said she contemplated about how the goddess despised her affection for Merlin from the beginning how she wanted all of Solana's attention when she was given the endowment from Vivian to become the vessel for the goddess. As Lady of the Lake Solana was responsible to stay true to the old ways to worship the goddess and her reign over the world. The goddess was just like mortals she was jealous of Solana's affection for Merlin. The goddess was a fraud she too felt self-doubt that was her true purpose for speaking with Solana. It was not that she was concerned about Solana's welfare or her broken heart.

Solana eyes grew wild and suddenly calm as she stopped crying and spoke in almost a whisper, I understand goddess I know your true purpose here. It is not that you are concerned it is that you want to make sure my loyalty still remains with you. You do not care about my feelings at all. You want to ensure that I will be faithful to you as your vessel on this world. Then Solana spoke in a loud voice filled with anger as she shouted out, "I denounce you goddess I denounce my servitude to you. I take back this wretched power and be gone from my eyes never to walk in my presents again!!!" Solana turns her back to the goddess and walks away. The goddess grew wide with anger as she listened to Solana growing more and more furious she roared back, "How dare you!!!! Solana you cannot denounce me you simpleton you are The Lady Of The Lake I am the only one who can endow or disallow you to be such only in death will you be able to leave these walls. You pledged your life to the Goddess and Avalon

now if you wish to denounce me and Avalon it will be by your death only my dear."
The goddess forged chains of gold as they sprouted from the ground latching on to Solana's leg she was unable to move as the ball and shackle tightened around her leg. The Goddess looked to Solana with disgust as she bellowed, "You are too proud I think you need to learn some humility my dear."
The goddess took Solana's beautiful face and distorted it, mutilating her skin to show a very horrible scar across her face. The scar was terrible it had ruined her once beautiful features the scar ran down the right side of her face and the goddess was still not satisfied with just that scar. "No I feel you need a bit more my dear." Solana begged for the goddess to stop but this did not phase her in the slightest The Goddess took Solana's marked face into her hands racked her fingers across the horrible wound to display pock marks and boils. "Now that is better my dear now you have to look at my handy work so that you may learn not to offend my delicate nature."
The goddess looked to the heavens as she did an exquisite golden framed mirror fell to her feet. Here Solana here is a gift from the gods so you may look upon yourself and remember your folly. Solana beautiful face was no more it was a horrible reminder of the wrath of the goddess.
From that moment on Solana swore she would dedicate her life to finding her beloved and ending the goddess hold over her and Avalon. Solana laid in wait and bided her time showing the goddess only her fake admiration earning her good graces again. Solana would sneak away to the caves below and seek the Book of Knowledge searching for a way to bring back Merlin and stop the

goddess once and for all. Solana search the scripts and looked through all the old scrolls for anything that would help her find Merlin. She studied the old incantations of Avalon and learned of a scared jewels that were brought to Avalon from Koldacot the jewels were hidden at three different temples of the Goddess of Avalon in case of war.

The jewels by themselves were harmless but once the three jewels were placed together in an intermittent way they would have the power to open portals between time and space. Solana read the script for the scroll and her eyes widen in excitement now she had a way to bring Merlin back. Solana took the old scroll from the catacombs and set out on her mission to find the jewels.

Each crystal held a special power. The first was a blue sapphire jewel which was known as the stone of destiny it would empower the beholder with control over the elements. The second was a pink jewel this was the stone of love. The jewel would empower the beholder with allure and vitality to make their hearts desire fall madly in love with them. The third and last jewel was the moon stone which glistens in color shimmering a pearl white. This stone would empower the beholder with the ability of foretelling the future and telepathy.

Each jewel is cut in a precise shape so that all three will combine to make a perfect diamond. The scroll said that once all three jewels are untied only one of pure heart will be able to wield its power to open portals in time and space. Solana wasted no time as she set out in search of the three jewels of time to form the diamond that would allow her to open the portal and bring Merlin back to her side once again.

Solana knew that it would not be easy to locate the three crystals. The task would require someone with skills which she did not possess. Solana sat and thought to herself **"who has the power to seek these jewels out for me?"**

**"What did the scroll mean one pure of heart? Where would the ancient hide these jewels and why?"** Solana was then hit with a brilliant idea she knew of only one who could help her in this task Helena. She was from the ancient world she would know of the scroll and the jewels.
**"Yes Helena would have to help me."** She said to herself.
Solana knew she would have to lead Helena into helping her without knowing her true reason to bring forth the jewels of time. Solana headed back to the atrium in the center of the room she stood focusing all her energy on Helena. Solana concentrated with all her might thinking about Helena.
Solana's half-moon started to glow as she continued on thinking about Helena. Solana called for the powers of Avalon to aid her to find Helena. It was like a flash of images raced through her thoughts she was drawn to the forest.
Helena stood there with a winged horse and Uther. Helena was trying desperately to place a bridle on the enormous animal. Uther stood in a daze as if under a spell. Solana look onward and realized that the winged horse was Pegasus the animal of legend.
**Solana remembered her father Magnus would speak of the animals of war in stories that would lull her to sleep but they were not real. By the Gods if what Solana was seeing were true then Helena means to wage war on Mt. Olympus itself!!!!!**

Uther what has happened to Uther why is he standing there so unaware of what is happening Solana wondered his eyes seem glazed over and this dumbfounded look upon his face wait what is that he is holding she saw in the distance a glimmer of bright blue in Uther's hand is that one of the jewels mentioned in the scroll. Yes I remember the blue sapphire Uther has one of the three pieces that are needed to bring Merlin back to me. I must seek them out and make haste heaven knows how long before they move on.

Solana was worried about her appearance now that the goddess had disfigured her face. Solana had no time to waste so she wrapped cloth around her head and face to mask her horrible scars as she raced to the veil between the worlds. Solana concentrated her energy focusing on the mist she placed her hand against the deep fog sending out impulses as she moved her hands in a circular motion the veil lifted. Solana raced to the shore with swift pace she knew she needed a horse being The Lady of the Lake has its advantages. Solana thought about her own *rounsey*, the chestnut brown beauty with black mane strong, agile, playful horse Solana kept thinking about her horse as she did off in the distance as if by the gods themselves appeared Solana's horse without hesitation she whisked herself on her stallion as she headed to the forest.

# CHAPTER THREE
# INGRIEN'S DISGRACE

Ingrien recently married to Garlois was coming to terms with being a queen of the land by the sea. Ingrien who was not used to all the pressures ventured out of the castle to seek guidance from her aunt on how to be a good queen.
Ingrien was now wife to Garlois who was putting undue tension on her to conceive a child. Ingrien still longed for Uther to her very soul she was tormented by her affection for him. Ingrien was unable to find a way to bring herself to consummate the marriage with Garlois.
Ingrien had avoided his advances and was finding it more and more difficult to find ways to counter Garlois's affections. She knew it was only a matter of time before she would have to submit to his will. Ingrien's aunt was to be forced into a marriage that she did not want. Ingrien knew she would be the only one that could understand her dilemma.
Ingrien summoned her hand maiden. The little timid meek girl enter her bed chamber the sweet innocent girl enter the room without a sound as Ingrien ordered her to fetch the royal carriage. The hand maiden bowed as she replied in a hushed tone, "right away my queen."
She headed out of the bed chamber down the wide hall outside to the courtyard toward the stables. The stables themselves housed

many great breeds of horse flesh. The hand maiden called to the stable boy, "fetch the royal carriage for the queen and be quick about it."
Ingrien hurried as she dressed wasting no time as she did not want to attract the attention of Garlois or the court. Ingrien hurried outside under the veil of early morning she raced to the carriage as she urge the driver to be swift but quite as they left the castle. Ingrien raced to her aunt's vassal of land.

 Ingrien always loved traveling out to the manor house away from the court and high society. She knew she could seek refuge let her guard down and truly be herself. Ingrien was at the manor house within a few hours as she stepped out of the carriage it was as if the history of her short lived life flash before her eyes.

Ingrien was transported back to her childhood the sights the memories were came flooding back. Her body filled with warmth as she became overjoyed with the splendor of it all. Ingrien began to wonder how her life veer so far from the many happy memories, why could she not live to fulfill her dreams. Ingrien's eyes filled with tears as she thought of her fate now plagued with her true love and her husband.

Uther was the one who was constantly in her thoughts conflicted by her duty to the kingdom and her infections heart why could they not be one in the same.
Ingrien approach the manor house as she walked in her aunt could sense right away that this visit was not going to be for pleasure but for pain. Ingrien was unable to look her aunt in the

eyes she was ashamed of her feelings she wanted advice but could not find the words to express it.

Ingrien's aunt immediately embraced her "dear one what troubles you so that causes this much pain?" Ingrien could not hold back the tears any longer as she blurted out, "Oh Aunt Heneretta my heart is torn my husband wants to consummate our marriage and produce an heir for the kingdom. I cannot find the strength to lay with him. I have evaded his advances for now but it is only a matter of time, what am I to do? My heart belongs to another as if it were written in the stars themselves. Please dear Aunt Heneretta please give me advice."
Ingrien's faced had redden and her eyes were becoming puffy with each tear that fell she was now crying uncontrollably
Heneretta was puzzled by her dear niece's plight but as she thought of her own experience it did make sense to her about Ingrien's own misfortune. Heneretta was also forced into marriage at a young age to a man she had never met to maintain the kingdom. The anguish she suffered and the torment of her own heart was in kind to Ingrien's situation now.

Heneretta was born in a time of great distress in the kingdom. The court was divided in two factions. They began to wage war against one another for control of the throne. The King was growing older and knew that it was time to name an heir. He was blessed with two sons Hershal and Bradgam.

Hershal was Heneretta's father as well as the rightful heir to the throne but his younger brother Bradgam had other plans for the

kingdom. The kingdom grew fruitful with peace. As the brothers grew up they drifted further and further apart dividing a wedge between the courts.
Hershal grew into a fine strapping man in the blink of an eye his broad shoulders and muscled physic drew all the maiden's attention.
Bradgam was not gifted with his brother's attributes he was a tall lanky fellow with no muscle tone at all. He face was course and long as well. Bradgam's hair was straggled and curly. Hershal's hair was fine flowing long brown mane.  Hershal had soon become of age to marry as he had the pick of the realm Hershal chose the most beautiful lady of the land. So after Hershal was wed the sweet union produced Heneretta.

 Hershal was overjoyed at the sight of Heneretta he raced to the king's chamber only to be met with tragedy as his beloved father had taken ill and was dying. Both the brothers raced to side of their dying father as he lay in his bed chamber with the last breath of life within him. The King whispered for the chamberlain to come fourth. The chamberlain came into the bed chamber with the last rights of the king.
The chamberlain took out the mighty scroll and began to read it aloud. I King of Cornwall do begeth the kingdom and all their in to Hershal to my other son Bradgam I beget the manor house, and name you commander of the king's army and all its contents. I wish you both happiness, peace and health in your lives. The King fell dead after the reading of the scroll. Bradgam became furious as the chamberlain read the scroll cursing his dying father for his wishes. Hershal knew that Bradgam would wage war to

gain control of the kingdom. Hershal first act as king was to have his brother taken to the castle dungeon before any harm befell his family.
The court mourned the death of the king months went by as Hershal found his footing as king of the lands. Hershal tried to lift the spirits of the court by starting the commencement of coronation. The Queen would not surrender the throne to Hershal until he released her son Bradgam from the dungeon upon his release Bradgam would be given his birthright of commander of the king's army.

Hershal could move forward with the coronation until the queen abdicated the throne. Hershal knew that releasing Bradgam would case war to ensue so he consulted his court advisors who advised him to make a pact with his brother to keep peace in the land. Hershal ponders the advice of the court knowing his brother's heart and lust for power he knows the best way to keep the peace was to give Bradgam an incentive he could not refuse.

Hershal knew that Bradgam wanted to marry and as king he would have to give his consent before any such union could take place. Hershal saw his opportunity for the kingdom to have peace. Hershal agreed to his mother's terms and degreed that his bother would only be released to his current station as prince he could only take his birthright when he was married.

Hershal knew he could delay his brother's plans to wed for 16 years when his newborn daughter would be of age to wed. The deed was done Hershal had his daughter's betrothal drawn up Heneretta fate was sealed. Bradgam wasted no time to take his place as commander immediately after he was released but to his dismay he was told of his fate degreed by the king. Bradgam knew it would be easy to find a bride so he agreed to the terms of his release thinking he outsmarted his brother little did Hershal know that Bradgam had a maiden he married before his father's death, waiting in the wings.

Bradgam had taken this maiden virtue and she had conceived a child. Bradgam hurried out of the castle as he raced to Ovella side. Ovella was a pretty slip of a girl her luminous hazel eyes, sweet pouty lips, strong robust body a vision of heaven that filled Bradgam heart with pride.

Ovella had taken a walk that afternoon as she saw off in the distance in the alcove near the castle a familiar horse riding up the lane towards her. Ovella was overwhelmed can it be true is that my prince no it cannot be for he is imprisoned in the castle by degree of the king. Bradgam spotted his breathtaking beauty and raced to her as he shouted her name, "Ovella Ovella..... She turn to his direction tears of disbelief streamed down her cheeks as she replied, "I am here my love my sweet prince." The horse came upon her in a thunderous gallop Bradgam dismounted in a flash his arms raised to embrace his beloved Ovella.

She ran to his inviting embrace as she moved in close to taste of his lips. "I thought it was over I thought my life was damned by the gods as I learned of your imprisonment." Bradgam wiped

Ovella tear strained face caressed her cheek as he lifted her chin to look deep within her warm hazel eyes.
"I too believe my fate was sealed but my mother sacrificed her title of queen to gain my freedom by the look of you my dear I am just in time. We must hurry and announce our marriage to the court little does my brother know we are married by degree from the king. He will have no choice but to honor our father's wishes Hershal will have to make me commander of the king's army!" Ovella looked to Bradgam with a triumphant pride in her eyes as she replied, "Then our plans of overthrowing him have not changed?" As she sneered in utter delight. Let us not waste time talking, husband let us make haste and put your plan into action!!!" Bradgam elevated Ovella on his strong powerful destriers he then mounted behind her and rode toward the castle. Ovella and Bradgam reached the castle by mid-day as they found court assembling. The prince headed toward the throne room where dinner was being arranged. "Good we have time to dress before dinner my dear let us adjourn to our bed chamber." Hershal was dressing for dinner feeling quite pleased with himself outsmarting his brother and foiling his plans. The queen was holding her sweet precious Heneretta in her arms cradling her close to her bosoms Heneretta cooed and giggled as a wry smile appeared on her face that was the last time happiness would ever grace her lips.
Bradgam and Ovella hurried to their bed chamber as they dressed for dinner. The court was all a flutter at the sight of the two of them hand in hand as they walked through the castle the spectacle of it was so vulgar. The Lords and Ladies mutter as they whispered and dissention fell among the court. The Prince and

his beloved headed to the front of the table on the right side of his dear mother Bradgam sat down with his bride next to his side. The court headed to their seats the trumpets sounded the room filled with silence as high king Hershal with his queen made their entrance. The court arose to greet them each bowing in the king's wake. The king and queen were seated at the head of the table. Mead was poured as foul and venison was served with a fish cake spiced mule wine was fragrant in the air as they dined. Everyone was enjoying the fellowship the Prince arose as he nodded to the minstrel to sound the music for he wanted to address the court. The minstrel strummed his liar loudly catching the attention of the whole court as they looked up to see the Prince standing at attention.
"Dear King Hershal and Queen Aguith Lord and Ladies of the realm it is my privileged to be in your presents this night. I would like to offer a toast to Hershal my dear brother congratulations on your ascension to the throne please raise your tankers
Lords and Ladies the court responded and raised their tankers in unison they replied, "May the gods bless you King Hershal" Bradgam continued to speak, "Also dear friends and family I would like to take this opportunity to introduce my wife Ovella." The court was in shock and awe as the words spilled from Bradgam's mouth.

Hershal face lost all its color as his frustration grew to hate Hershal, he stood up straight as a shot as he shouted at the top of his lungs, "THIS MARRIAGE IS A FARCE I did not give permission under our chivalrous code you are a fool brother there is no marriage here and never will be. I do not care how many

bastard children you create your marriage must be approved by the King.
 Bradgam stood unyielding by his brother's word as he replied, "Bother are you quite finished I would dare not interrupt the King. Hershal was at a loss for words his brother stood in the wake of his outburst unaffected at all in a confused tone Hershal replied, "I am finished" Bradgam stood with sheepish grin on his face as he continued
"It is true brother I must have approval from the King to wed. That is why I was able to marry Ovella.  Dear brother for I had our late father's permission to marry. Now that you are aware I am in accordance with our chivalrous code. You dear brother must honor your part of the truce with our mother. It is time to bestow upon me my birthright as commander of the king's army dear brother."
Hershal growing more and more anger with every word utter by his brother, he knew his goose was cooked. He had to think of a way to stall. *Hershal think... I got it.*

Hershal stood once more, "I will not speak of such matters here and now it is not the time brother dear to discuss such matters Now is a time to eat and drink in the celebration of our united kingdom minstrel music the hall was in a hushed silence as the brothers both sat down all the court was uneasy based on the events of the evening all dined in a quite silences as they headed off to their quarters.
Hershal bought some time but not much he knew his plans were laid to ruin within the blink of an eye. Hershal was overcome with so many questions.

How could father give his permission on such a union? Why they were not married in a church among the court? Why was Bradgam trying to hide this from everyone? Hershal think what can I do to reel my treacherous brother into my trap to keep the kingdom united? Hershal agonized over this till the wee hours of the morn when he had an epiphany "Yes I have it instead of a betrothal between Heneretta and Bradgam I will pair her with his first born and the alliance will be forged from the two of them peace will rein throughout."

The plan was set in motion now to make sure there were no surprises. Hershal would call upon the dark powers of the druids in the forest to make the prophecy he would call upon the druids to curse his brother to ensure he would never see his birthright fulfilled.

Hershal went deep within the depths of the castle just beyond the armory Hershal walked towards the massive hearth where the hard iron was forged. Hershal continued to walk in the hearth and felt patterns of stones to open a passage to the forest tunnels to the middle of the druid's forest. Deep within the tunnel Hershal had revealed another secret stone pattern this was very enteric unlike the first stone pattern which was opened when all the stones were touched this new pattered required more.

Hershal pricked his finger letting the blood pool in the center of his hand he placed the pooled blood on the stone as the blood trickled down this snakelike trail throughout the stones began to glow and open another passage into a dark hallow in the middle of the forest. Hershal stood in the middle of the druid's safe hold as he treaded light on his feet the druids heard him and sensed an intruder among them. Hershal began to chant the forked tongue language of the druids "tera hulta meno young wizards of old I call upon you to appear."

Hershal called them to come forth as he placed his hands on the center stone as the blood from his hand poured down the stone Hershal called to the four winds the sky grew dark as rain fell a flash of lighten struck the center stone causing fire to light the Earth sending a signal to the druids. The druids were forest people who lived by the goddess and nature. They were an old race of people comprised of several factions the bards were the keepers of the wisdom tradition.

They memorized the key material of the tradition, much of which was put into poetic form and made it available to the people. The Ovates were the shamans of the community. Among their duties was the establishment of contact with ancestors in the spirit realm. They also engaged in divination of various kinds, including the reading of entrails, in attempts to predict the future.

The Druid priests were the most powerful leaders in the community. They presided over worship and group ceremonies, and often served as advisors to the secular rulers.

The Druid religion was nature-based and its worship cycle was marked by the movements of the Sun and Moon. The year was marked by the changing positions of the rising sun, the solstices, equinoxes, and the four additional festivals halfway between these four that marked important points in the agricultural seasons. These were known by different names in different locations and at different times.

Through blood for many of the royal grasp the powers of the goddess two of the high druid priests were brothers to the king. With a rush of wind the druids appeared to see Hershal standing in their wake. "Why have you call upon us Hershal?"

Hershal fell to his knees and exclaimed, "I am in need of the power of the goddess to sustain our kingdom I pray to the druids it is time to evoke the spirit of the dragon to have peace throughout the land and have no bloodshed. I need your foresight brothers to ensure the truce within the kingdom. I call upon my druid brethren the fate of our kingdom is in your hands."
The druids looked to one another with and replied, "Tis true that the fate of the kingdom is at stake but the goddess will decide if it is worthy of our powers we will call upon her to find if your request is admirable!"

The druid priests bent down in unison to took the moist earth and spread it all over their bodies. They each took out a dagger and tore at their flesh causing a bead of blood in their right hand. With their left hand they held it out palm side up to capture a pool of rain water.

Once the water was gathered the druids in one fast motion clasp hands together. As their hands touch they swayed with the wind chanting to the goddess the force of the druid's energy shook the Earth beneath them. The wind began to howl as the sea waves crashed against the cliffs. The sky turned a vivid shade of blue as the moon began to glow bright white the clouds opened as the goddess appeared within the shadows of the night sky. The goddess looked down upon the druids as she spoke to their minds eye for her voice would have killed them in an instant. "Why do you call upon me?" The druids replied in unison, "Mistress we require your foresight for our beloved kingdom it is at a crossroads oh goddess will you lend us aid."

The goddess responded, "Yes I will, I see people divided I see treacherous intent in the family soul. New birth brings forth a truce but it comes at a price. Talks of peace but war in their hearts a marriage forced where both parties are enemies. I see another in the mists of time he will be a great king but will have a short reign from the fruit of his lions will give a daughter whose heartbreak will bring fourth an evil on the land. This daughter will also bear a son who will heal the land."

The goddess became weary and withered away in the winds. The druids told of the goddess foresight. Hershal knew he must ask the druids for a potion to put his mind at rest which would seal the fate of the kingdom. Brother's I call upon your aid I must ask for the potion of death the druids eyes widen at the sound they heard uttered from Hershal lips.

Their demeanor changed as they focused on what Hershal required. The druid priest responded, "You know what you ask if we provide the potion of death there is a price that must be paid!!!"

Hershal looked to the druids with intensity in his eyes, "I know but I have no other choice it is a small price to pay if it ensures peace and I would be proud to pay it."

"Very well Hershal we will grant your request the debt will be your first born son to be sacrificed to the life of a druid. Hershal knew the price with my blood oath I agree and his blood dropped on the stone. As soon as his blood hit the stone as the druids pooled their energy to summon the power of the Earth they called upon Lucifer for aid to take the water from the river Stixx. The water born of death and tears of the grieving. The druids pulled the toadstools from the ground two of the druids ran out to the sea as they called the mermaids to shore for their scales. All components were collected as they met back at the center stone where they call upon the wind formed a funnel of whirling wind to mix all the potion together.

The druids called to the dwarfs of the forest for a glass vile to hold the death potion in. Hershal was given the vile he took great care as he headed back to the castle. At last Hershal could rest his weary head knowing full well he would set the wheels to motion for peace in the kingdom.

Hershal called the court to assemble that morning to unleash his plan. Hershal called for Prince Bradgam the prince arose ready to combat his brother s Ovella let out a horrible cry. Water and blood fell to the floor as Ovella stood hunch over, it is time Bradgam the baby is coming hand maiden came to Ovella's aid as she went into a hard labor with Bradgam newborn baby. Bradgam raced down to the great hall to meet Hershal at the ready to defend his marriage and status in the kingdom. Hershal was calm and speaking with the court as Bradgam had arrived "Ah Bradgam what kept you my dear brother I am ready to decree your birthright and name you commander of the king's army."

Bradgam was in awe of what his brother utter from his lips, "What brother I thought after your outburst last night I was in for a fight thank you King Hershal I shall not disappoint you. I accept my birthright."

Just as Bradgam was about to receive his birthright a meek simple girl enter the great hall and shouted, "Prince Bradgam you are the father of a strapping boy" Bradgam fell to his knees and thanked the gods for his good fortune not only was he given his birthright but he was father of the heir to the throne.

Bradgam called to the minstrels to strum their harps to the heaven "fill the room with mulled wine and lets us celebrate this good news." Hershal was overjoyed to hear about the birth of the new heir his plan was starting to take effect "Brother Come and share this joy with me let us drink and be merry." Hershal had a few moment of happiness as he laid in wait for the right moment to poison his brother drink and send him to Hades forever.

"Dear brother let us unite our kingdom forever on this blessed day. I purpose a royal decree that your new born son and my daughter will betrothal to wed on their 16th birthday. What say you good prince Bradgam." Bradgam did not dare challenge the king in front of the court so he gave his consent knowing full well that he would be king once he plotted the king's army to attack and kill Hershal on the morrow

"Brother I agree we must unite my son and heir will marry Heneretta on their 16 birthday." Hershal was overjoyed his plan was working flawlessly as he motioned the servant to bring to flagon's of mead Hershal reach down in his waistcoat pocket and grabbed the death potion as he was distracting Bradgam as he pour the vile of death into the flagon of mead and handed it to his brother. "Come Brother let us drink and be merry."

The court danced and drank into the hours of the morn before they adjourned to their quarters as the evening was coming to close Bradgam headed towards his en-suite to behold his new born son.

Bradgam just reached the outside of the door as his body grew cold the hall began to spin wildly. He heard his heartbeat race his eyes became transfixed and blurred. Bradgam's body trembled uncontrollably at first he threw it was too much drink but this was different somehow suddenly he lost his breath as he gasp for air a surge of burning raged through his body blood spouted out of his mouth and eyes.

Bradgam fell to the floor with a loud thud right outside his newborn son's door. He died as death took upon him from this world forever never to look upon his son, Bradgam cursed his brother name and family with his dying breath.

Hershal had retired from the celebration early for he knew tragedy would strike that night. Hershal lay in and out of sleep waiting for the moment when he would hear the grave news about Bradgam.

As Hershal was drifting off to sleep once more His body raised straight up in his bed haunted by the feeling his brother was dead. Hershal began to hear Bradgam's new born crying in the en-suite.

The newborn babe could sense that his father was ripped from this world. The babe lay crying the wet nurse headed down the hall with candle in hand to see what cause the babe to cry so loudly.

They walked softly down the hall as the light from the candle caught a glimpse of Bradgam lifeless body lying on the floor next to the ensuite of his new born son. The wet nurse thought that Bradgam had celebrated too hard and passed out on the floor. The wet nurse bent down to see the crimson red blood pooled next to Bradgam's face as she turn the body over to her horror Bradgam face was enlarged and his eyes bulged out of his head and blood poured out of his mouth onto her gown. The wet nurse let out a shrieking blood curling scream as she realized that Prince Bradgam was dead.

The guards came running down the hall as the lords and ladies lay asleep in their bed chambers unmoved. The guards saw their fallen commander. The head knight told the guards to search the grounds to find the assailant. The knight knew his duty was to inform the King. The knight headed to the King's bed chamber.

As the knight approached he grew more and more frighten about the King's reaction to the dire news. The knight traded lightly as he reached the solid oak door to the King's bed chamber. The knight knocked on the massive oak door the king's page stuck his head out the door. "What is the meaning of this disturbance? Do you know what time it is knight the king is at rest?" The knight looked at the lowly page with frustration "I am a knight of the realm page remember yourself when you address me I must speak with the king I have grave news wake him at once do not fuse about."

The page moved quickly to the bed and gently shook the king. Hershal arose with admit displeasure he held the page in his arms and shook him about. "WHAT IS IT?" Why are you disturbing my slumber what is the meaning of this well out with it boy?"

The scared page uttered, "There is a knight in the hall that must speak with you sir." The King Arose in a fury tossing the bed curtain a-rye. The King raced to the door knowing full well what was waiting for on the other side.

The king prepared his composure and set the stage for his performance the knight bowed to the floor not wanting to lock eyes with the king. "Sir forgive me your grace I have grave news of the prince. Sir the prince was struck down dead in the hall this night." The king blurted out, "by the gods no!" the king tore at his clothes and cry out, "my dear brother gone from this world. No this cannot be true Bradgam never had a chance to hold his dear babe. What horror is this that the Gods of this world inflict such pain upon our family first my beloved father and now my brother the pain is too much for any one man to bear." Tears welled up into the kings eyes as he sobbed deeply the king fell to the floor. "Help me knight take me to my brother I must see him."

The knight aided the king as they walked to the bed chamber where his brother's body lay. Bradgam lay lifeless in a pool of blood right outside the door of his new born. The sight would send a weaker man into shock but knowing the outcome the king was not fazed by the sight. Call for the royal apothecary and barber to remove and prepare my brother for a hero's funeral. The knight looked perplexed "Sir he did not die by the sword he died by the fates he is not entitled to a hero's funeral sir." The king became furious, "YOU DARE CORRECT ME KNIGHT? I am the king and I will say how my brother will be grieved not you by the gods or not my brother was a hero to this kingdom now away with you before I make an example out of your impertinence the knight left in disgrace to fetch the apothecary and barber.

The brother stood in the hall alone many things ran through Hershal's mind the debt has been assess and now the payment must be paid my unborn son placed into druid service but that was another day. The princess was overwrought with exhaustion after giving birth Hershal would break the grave news of Bradgam's death in the morn. Hershal retired and drifted off to sleep.

The next morn the princess awoke to greet her new born babe only to learn that he dear husband Bradgam was dead. The princess was sent over the edge. She was in disbelief she called to the knight you lie and continued to scream at him with hysterics until she fainted from all the excitement. The king arose with contentment and happiness for the kingdom future was sealed with the death of his brother. The court was still jovial at the news of the new born son of the prince Bradgam Hershal wasted no time as he announced the engagment of Heneretta to Bradgam son. The court was overjoyed to the King was sanctifying the kingdom with the marriage of the cousins. Plans were made for the burial of Bradgam as the others readied themselves for the funeral. The kings knights had went to the wood and prepared a pyre for the funeral Bradgam was dressed in ceremonial armor and carried by the knight's guard King Hershal and the Queen followed by princess, son, lords and ladies of the court. The King gave a detailed speech about the commander of the kings army that gave the court measures of grief and utter sadness filled the air as they cantor lit the pyre as Bradgam was sent on to his reward ash and smoke filled the air as Bradgam soul was lifted to Mt. Olympus as his ties to earthly plane were forever severed. His treachery lurked in the mist as his curse permeated the land with his grief stricken widow's tears the curse was sealed forever. The court watched as the fire engulf Bradgam the burning embers stood in it distance

Heneretta was doomed to a marriage she did not want forged to hold a kingdom by blood Heneretta's brother stolen from her and given to the druids. Heneretta's life was filled with nothing but anguish and strife.

Heneretta mother gave birth to a sister as well one of lustrous beauty. She was born free to marry as she choose. A feat that was not afforded to her. Heneretta despise her sister for that and her feelings ~~feeling~~ towards her sister would always be that of hate.

Heneretta thought if she abdicated from the throne her sister would also be forced to marry but it was to no avail the king favored Heneretta's sister over her in every way and would not relinquish Henrietta from her betrothal, on her 16th birthday she was forced to marry the prince. The prince was given every indulgence from his mother he was never disciplined as he grew older he become more and more selfish. The prince forced his affection on Heneretta raping her at his will as well as her ladies in waited.

One of the ladies in waiting fought back in the struggle she had struck the prince in the
 Head landing a massive vase on his crown that struck his skull cracking his head open as he fell to the bed the prince landed on

his neck breaking it. The prince died in their bed chamber from a broken neck the maiden was hanged in front of the court and Heneretta was banished from the court forever.

As her sister took her rightful place upon the throne the king's house was forever cursed after that. No son would be born to either sister Heneretta was barren and her sister gave birth to only one child Ingrien. Heneretta was one of the royal family so she was sent to live out her day at the manor house. Heneretta did find love and married a common man. Ingrien now stood on the threshold of the same terror her aunt befell. Ingrien longed for a simple life she never wanted to be queen. Ingrien knew it was her duty to fulfill her family's obligation but she dreaded every day in the castle. She looked for ways to leave the solace of the woods the beauty of the gardens. Heneretta had little advice to give.

Heneretta looked to her niece with sorrow in her eyes, "Dear child love come over time things happen in life and your heart dear one will grow into love. When you see Garlois's commitment to you when he stands by you during illness, childbirth, and your golden years. Ingrien you must give your heart to him. You must submit lay with him and produce an heir for our family continue the kingdom. Let it flourish in peace."

Ingrien left with a heavy heart as she ponder what her aunt had told her. Ingrien came to terms with her fate. **Now is not the time to be selfish. I am not a girl any longer with fanciful dreams I am queen as I queen I am expected to produce an heir. It is time I did what it is expected of me.**

Ingrien entered the manor house a mere babe in the woods as she left that day she exited a queen. Ingrien headed back to the castle once she returned Garlois was waiting for her.

Garlois was furious with her leaving the safety of the castle. As soon as she entered Garlois rushed to her side and embraced her. Then in his enraged state he began to shout "WHAT DID YOU THINK I WOULD NOT NOTICE YOU WERE GONE!!!! I have agonized for hours I sent the knights out looking for you. I prayed to the gods you were safe. Ingrien you are the only treasure that has value to me I hold you dear to my heart. I would be nothing without you Ingrien I am so angry with you right now to take such liberties with no regard for others you are so careless."

Ingrien stood and listened to Garlois rant about her absence the ferocity of him his passion for her was awe-inspiring for him to take such care when he could have easily just beaten her for her insolence as her father did she was impressed although his words did sting it was something to behold. "Yes Garlois you are right it was dumb for me to venture out without an escort. I know it was careless of me but I needed to see my aunt she is the only family I have."

Garlois knew she had suffered with the loss of her parents and was humbled by her words as he spoke softly to her, "Why could we not go together Ingrien or perhaps invite them here in the safety of the castle walls."

Ingrien sensed his humble tone of voice she was touched by his canter and understanding as she replied, "Garlois I have never been a wife to anyone. I have never laid with anyone before. I had to speak with her because she is the only person I have to seek advice on these matters."

Ingrien I know you are a noble women I will not take you against your will. Ingrien why not talk to me I am here for you. Sweetheart you are driving me insane your beauty fills my heart I want to drink in your kisses I want to taste of your tenderness. Ingrien I am just a man I have needs. I long for you many of the court are whispering about us how we have not yet produced an heir." Ingrien was outraged at what she was hearing, "The courts is whispering about us they fear the line will die out do they." Her eyes widens as her face became flushed "It is time Garlois we have no time to waste. You are right you have waited long enough."

Garlois ears perked up at Ingrien's words his eyes widen in delight as he grinned from ear to ear in eagerness. Garlois drew Ingrien close to him Ingrien's eyes filled with fear as her body trembled in response Garlois pressed his lips to hers. Ingrien's heart began to race.

Garlois moved his massive hand feeling her bountiful breast as they lay locked in her bodice. Ingrien's body quivered as a sudden jolt of heat pierced through her.
Garlois reached downward and started to unravel her corset as the corset fell to the floor a cold air moved across Ingrien's breast as

they fell forward making her flesh hard and ripen before his eyes. Garlois with his free hand had quickly undone his blecks to reveal his long hard shaft eager to enter his awaited treasure.

Ingrien looked down to see this massive stiff hard flesh. Garlois bent down and lifted Ingrien in his arms as he carried her to their bed chamber. Garlois stroked her hard ripen breast sending Ingrien into sure delight. Garlois gently place her on the bed where he started to caress her and fondle her luscious body.

 Ingrien was in uncharted territory all these new feeling the heat of the moment his soft hands touching her his lips kissing her sent her into pure ecstasy. Ingrien was excited and afraid at the same time. She tried to hold on to her virtue to fight against carnal pleasures but she was unable to. Ingrien submitted to her wanting lustful nature Garlois thrust his harden flesh into her. Tears of innocents fell from her eyes as Garlois tore into her. Ingrien screamed in pain at first and then with pure delight every time she gasp she would tighten around Garlois long hard shaft. The excitement the thrill of ecstasy overtook Garlois as he released his massive manhood into Ingrien.

She lay in the bed with her tear stained face as her innocents pour out red crimson blood stained the bed clothes. Garlois looked to his beloved as he reached out his hand to hold her face.
 Garlois wiped the tears from her face and expressed his love for her once again. "Ingrien my love you behold my desire. I must rest dear heart for you have taken my heart and soul. Let us rest and bask in the joy of each other." Ingrien lay her head on his

broad chest as they fell asleep in each other's embrace. Ingrien pondered what just happened she asked the gods, "Why they torment her? Why must she be cursed? I love Uther even now as I lay beside Garlois I still long for Uther. I feel nothing for Garlois. I must turn my back on my heart I have to focus on my duty as queen and wife for the sake of the kingdom. This I vow I will forever forsake my heart and my love for Uther. Ingrien knew with the loss of her virtue she would be disgraced in the eyes of the gods because she did not give herself fully to Garlois. He took pleasures in her body but her heart and her soul would belong to Uther forever.

**Comment [BP]:**

# CHAPTER FOUR
# SOLANA'S STRATAGEM

She had no time to waste but Solana had to be careful not to arouse attention of the goddess. Solana astride her mighty horse and she knew no matter how fast she rode it would never be fast enough to catch up with Uther and Helena. Solana knew she had to delve into her powers to transport herself directly to Uther and Helena before they moved on. Solana rode back to Avalon as she crept down to the catacombs deep in the heart of Avalon she focused her energy on Uther in the wooded glen.

Solana concentrated on the sapphire the first of the three jewels of time. She could feel the magi within her grow as the half-moon in her forehead started to glow bright white. The light began to grow around her in this white luminous ball encompassing her. The bubble around her moved into the air like a flash as she was transported to the wooded glen. Helena was turned about ready to leave with Pegasus. Solana's eyes widen she rubbed her eyes to make sure she was not seeing things. She could not believe her eyes as she saw this magnificent animal of legend. Pegasus massive wings glowed in the sunlight shimmer pear white, Pegasus stood as the tallest horse Solana had ever seen Pegasus had to be 18 hands high. Solana was in awe as she saw his spiraled golden horn. Solana bowed to the ground Pegasus saw Solana bowing out of the corner of his eyes as he turned, "Finally some respect from a mortal."

Helena was puzzled with Pegasus remark as she turned to see Solana lady of the lake bowing. Helena rushed to see why Solana would venture from the safety of Avalon to the wooded glen. Helena raised her hand in the air waving "Solana is that you? Why are you wearing a veil? To what do we owe the pleasure of your present's lady of the lake?" Solana at the sight of Pegasus was dumbfounded and at a loss for words. Helena growing agitated with Solana non response beckon, "Come... come.... now Solana why are you here what has brought you to the forest lady of the lake?" Solana knew she had to be cunning with her answer to not lead on to her ultimate goal. I am communing with nature Helena revitalizing my commitment to the Goddess. Pegasus became enraged as he shouted, "THE GODDESS IS NOTHING BUT A SPOILED LITTLE CHILD OF THE GODS. Who are about to receive their ends over the land as we reunited the animals of war. They will pay for what they have done. We will wreak havoc on Mt. Olympus and end the god's tyranny once and for all!"

Solana could not believe what she was hearing. "What you are waging war with the gods?" Pegasus looked to Solana as he simply said, "Yes" Solana questioned Pegasus "The gods created you they gave us life how could you turn on your creator like that?" Pegasus was unmoved by Solana's questions as he sarcastically replied, "How indeed the gods imprisoned myself and my family because we posed a threat to them. The gods doomed us to horrors you could never imagine. They will pay for their deeds." Helena interjected, "Pegasus she does not need to know this Pegasus she's a vessel for the goddess lady of the lake pledged to protect the veil between worlds." Uther motionless in the forest awaiting Helena's commands. "Helena is that Uther over there in the distance?"

Helena had to think fast before Solana knew the truth about Uther and the spell he was under "Yes it is he is on a quest. Solana why are you covering your face if you are communing with nature? We must take our leave Solana we are in a hurry to go. " "Helena I would like to speak to Uther about a matter of urgency" Solana approach Uther's direction Helena shouted, "STOP Solana do not force me to harm you."

Solana turned and giggled, "You harm me I am the lady of the lake less you forget Helena. You cannot harm me I am a vessel of the goddess. How dare you threaten me? "
Helena called upon the powers of the Earth as Solana moved closer to Uther.

The ground quaked and shook under Solana's feet as she lifted her foot and moved toward Uther the Earth below became brittle and opened to swallow Solana in a colossal cavern. Solana clawed and reached for something to stop her decent.

Helena looked to Pegasus, "Hurry we must flee now before she escapes." Helena was is the rush. Pegasus mockingly stated, "she is trapped deep within the Earth there is no need to fear her she's a mere mortal." Helena knew that Solana was magi she possessed powers as the goddess vessel who would lend her protection.

"Trust me Pegasus we must flee for it is only a matter of time before she escapes. Besides we do not need the goddess finding out about our plan of revenge." Before Helena could finish her thought Solana burst out of the cavern on a geyser of white water.

"You will pay for that Helena." Solana called to the four winds a flash of fireballs came from the skies aimed at Helena and Pegasus. Helena has no time to react. Pegasus with his mighty wings began to fan the wind the sheer force of blew out the fireball before they had a chance to impact.
The smoldering balls of coal and ash hit the ground and dissipated as dust filled the air shielding Pegasus and Helena. Uther remained unmoved.

Solana knew Uther was under a spell Solana shouted, "Helena I know you are a formidable opponent it would be pointless to battle I am aware of your spell on Uther. Your plans to overthrow Mt. Olympus. I too seek vengeance against the gods. Solana uncovered her disfigured face. Look at me look at what that vile witch the goddess has done to me. I want to join you in your cause. I was forced into to service to the goddess I have unsettled anger as well."

Helena was shocked to see the hideous horror of Solana's face but still did not know if Solana was speaking the truth. "How can I be certain this is not a ploy of the goddess Solana?" Enraged at Helena Solana ironically declared, "Helena if I was here for the goddess I would have attacked you on site I am here on my own accord Helena let me join you I can help in your quest."

Helena looked to Pegasus for his take on this recent development. "Pegasus what do you think?" Pegasus replied, "I do not know if we can trust her yet but if she tries in any way to dissuade our plans I will kill her. Now let us be on our way."

Helena motioned Solana to join them as they headed onward to the sea. Solana knew the only way to search for the stones of power was to join Helena in her quest. She knew that she would have to be sly to find out the information she required without giving away her own true plans. Solana wanted to gather the stones of power to find her beloved Merlin and bring him back to her.

"Why are we headed to the seaside Helena?" We are going there to release the Phoenix from her imprisonment. You don't mean the mythical phoenix do you? Yes the very same Helena explained the true story behind the mythical creature to Solana.

You see Solana the Phoenix was a beautiful women with scarlet red and blond hair her beauty was known far and wide throughout the land. Her beauty would be a downfall for it was said that the Phoenix was more beautiful than the goddess. This enraged the goddess to be compared to a mortal.

The goddess tried to burn the beautiful mortal known as the Phoenix. Zeus saw what the goddess was trying to do so he intervened as the Phoenix was set ablaze with the fire of the gods Zeus sent down his massive thunderbolt causing the beautiful maiden to embrace the fire and transform into this massive winged bird. The giant firebird soared to the heaven and stood beside Pegasus and the other animals of war. As a titian for the gods the Phoenix would set ablaze to villages leaving ash and smoke in its wake. If a mortal would to look upon the Phoenix their eyes would burn out rendering them to be blind. The Phoenix song would make mortal's ears bleed. "We are releasing her? How are we to release her and where is she?" Pegasus interjected, "the Phoenix is held captive deep in the sea unable to see the sun rays feel the warmth of the Earth. The sweet wind on her back all she has known is darkness and despair locked in the depths of the sea. She is enclosed in impenetrable cube encased with chains. The cube is bolted down with granite weights forged by Poseidon who keeps constant vigil to make sure the Phoenix does not escape."

Solana looked at Pegasus in disbelief, "How are we even to have a chance at setting her free with all those obstacles ahead of us?" Pegasus remarked, "These are mere trifles with my power Helena had Uther the pure heart as well as yourselves it should be easy for us to rescue the Phoenix. After all you are the Lady of the Lake aren't you? Solana you have power over the element of water as demonstrated only moments ago."

Solana knew very little about her power as she was growing into her service to the goddess. She had not fully tested her abilities only in bouts of pure rage has she ever been able to harness her power. Solana did not want to let on that she was unskilled but she also did not want Pegasus, Helena and Uther to depend on her alone to rescue the Phoenix. Solana replied, "Yes I am the Lady of the Lake Pegasus but I am not the Lady of the sea I fear you put too much faith in me." Pegasus began to laugh, " No my dear one you misunderstand with our power combined is the only way we will be able to free the Phoenix Helena was in full agreement as she interjected, "Solana we have to pool our powers together Uther is the only one who can break the harden steel chains with Excalibur and the stone of power." Solana was relieved to hear that the weight was lifted off of her shoulder as they shared the rescue together. "Oh I see that does put my mind at ease Helena you mentioned the stone of power. What is the stone of power?

Helena forgot that Solana was unaware about the jewels of time as she replied, "Oh Solana the jewels of time are precious stones that are scattered to the four winds as a precaution so that they would not fall into the wrong hands it is rumored that if all stones are combined the power they create will give the bearer the ability beyond the gods themselves to travel through time and space itself. Abilities over humans and animals alike. Solana was intrigued as she replied, "Wow Helena I had no idea such power existed." Helena looked to Solana with caution, "The jewels of time are not of this world they were brought here by Merlin's people to be used under great peril to protect against the gods.

Where is Merlin? I thought he would have intervened by now seeing as we how we have Uther helping on our plans."

Merlin was still in the future with the goddess as he drank of her the memories that flooded his mind. The horrible war, the lost, Norwich rage engulfed him with one thought to seek vengeance against Desmoria.

Visions of Ursula on her deathbed the creation of Stonehenge his fortress of solitude. Images of his sweet Solana as a rush of warmth overtook Merlin his heart started to quicken. He became flush at the thought of Solana. The goddess lay in his arms kicking and struggling as Merlin drank. He cast the goddess aside as he centered his attention on Desmoria whereabouts. Merlin concentrated all his energy on Desmoria honing in on her location. Merlin was hit with a jolt of electricity his eyes grew wide as he spotted the villainous bitch Desmoria on the hunt for her next conquest of servant girls.

Merlin locked eyes with her as loud shriek was sounded from Desmoria's lips, urging the coachmen "Hurry... hurry we must make haste to the castle." The coachmen set horses and returned to the castle. She knew Merlin had followed her but she thought of him as no threat because of his head injury.

Demoria/Ezerbeth always hedged her bets she lay a protection spell around the castle to make sure her food source was safe. She had been quite busy gathering enough blood to feed her for decades. Desmoria/Ezerbeth had a great scheme to acquire her food supply. She went to outlining areas in search of servants for her castle.

Desmoria/Ezerbeth would gather young girls of birth giving age. She made promises to the families of the girls that she would cultivate their daughters into court. She would gather girls at first and then later she would gather men that tickled her fancy she took them to the castle. Desmoria/Ezerbeth would make it look as though the servants displeased her. Desmoria/Ezerbeth would punished them and send them to the dungeon.

Desmoria/Ezerbeth would then exact unspeakable horrors to procure the most blood from her victims. She would bathe in the crimson shower of blood as it covered her from head to toe. All the servants feared her and would not dare speak a word against her,rumors spread throughout the castle about the disappearance of the servants many would whisper blood countess under their breath as Desmoria/Ezerbeth walked the halls covered in the blood of the innocent servants that were just a mere snack for this villainous bitch. She was stunned by the sight of Merlin. She knew it was time to lay her defenses because Merlin was coming for her to seek his justice at the onslaught of the brutal mayhem Desmoria/Ezerbeth has caused when she killed Norwich in cold blood. She knew that she would have to be more cautious now. Desmoria/Ezerbeth began to immerse herself into the occult learning protection spells. She wanted to protect her food supply at all costs. Merlin concentrated on Desmoria to find her whereabouts he used his mind's eye to link with Desmoria.

Merlin focused his power to see a figure of regal women small in stature with an immaculate body snow white skin encoring full breasts muscular rounded legs with a slim waste and long chestnut brown hair.

Something was wrong because he was focusing on Desmoria yet this woman comes to his mind. Merlin was puzzled by this for a moment as he realized she must be in disguise to assimilate in the new time. Well Merlin tried to look at the surroundings to gain his bearings. He looked upon a huge mountain range where nestled in a lush emerald valley stood a monumental castle of ivory white towers reaching to the skies. **I must move quickly she can sense me looking for her I have to transport myself there now!!!!** Merlin stood on the ruins of Avalon as he gathered his power moving his hands in a circular motion building his transportation spell fixating his mind's eye on the ivory white castle.

The spell was growing in power as Merlin body began to shake as a surge of power flashed through his body which engulfed him in a glowing orange hue as a bubble immersed him. He jettison into the air like a fireball from the heavens.

Merlin raced over fields and glen, magnificent forests, huge mountain ranges were a blur flowing rivers and raging seas. Merlin was overwhelmed with the sure growth in the landscape over a few hundred years. He was just outside of the castle high in the Carpathian Mountains as he scurried down the mountain side.

Merlin stood outside the castle gates unable to move forward. Merlin walked around the castle circling unable to enter. Merlin tried with all his might only to be met with a force field that sent him flying as if he was hit by a thunderbolt from Zeus himself.

His body arched as he collided with the hard jagged rock his back took the brunt of the blow as he fell to the ground. Merlin was stunned for a moment as he gathered his facilities and stood upright. Merlin contemplated for a moment, "**Ah I see she has been busy with her time. She has laid down defenses. Desmoria is formidable enemy she has sought out the ways of the magi.**"

Merlin was depleted from the transportation spell he was not ready for Desmoria/Ezerbeth. Merlin knew his best course of action was to build his energy. He must return to his fortress of solitude. Merlin must journey to stone of power to build his strength up. **I must try to return to the stones of power.** He knew he had just enough strength to return. Merlin tried to transformed into his dragon form he was unable to do so. He used the last bit of energy to levitate into the skies looking for the stones of power. Merlin levitated until he saw out of the corner of his eyes the familiar stones glyphs covered in a thick mist of fog concealing it from the eyes of the mortals. Merlin landed as almost fully drained of energy Merlin tried to lift the veil between worlds.

Merlin with all the strength he had left raised his hands into the air. He moved them in a cross motion to lift the veil of thick dense fog as his hands crossed and moved downward the veil lifted. Through the years the stones of power were in decade the once glorious monoliths were in disarray the mighty stone alter was turned to rubble and ruin.

Merlin was distraught at the sight of his once beloved fortress he did all he could do, Merlin fell to his knees threw his hands into the air in utter disbelief and frustration tears began to weld up in his eyes as he cried out , "WHY? How could this happen? What could cause this? Tears streamed down his face as he sobbed uncontrollability he looked to the heavens with rage in his eyes as he shouted, "HOW COULD YOU LET THIS HAPPEN. Gods you aren't special to take from others and turn your backs when they need you." Merlin knew it was pointless to dwell on he had to reach the stones of power to recharge himself.

Merlin slowly walked as he reached the outer edge of the stones of power as he reach his arms out to each side of the gigantic stone pliers his body become infused by magnificent colors of flashing light. Merlin was lifted into the air as his body floated to the center of the stones. It circles his body and bathed it in the power of the magi. He was rendered unconscious as Norwich and Ursula's spirits appeared.

Norwick looked to Merlin with amazement "Ursula look how he has aged our once young man's has turned old and gray like the turning of a page. Ursula interjected, "Merlin traveled through time steam that is why he aged my dear. Remember dear heart we are not of this world as you and I have found out it takes its toll

Merlin has experienced a side effect due to his madness of running after Desmoria in the time stream.

He was wanting to avenge your death. Merlin leapt in after her and fell through the time stream thus aging him." Norwick responded, "Yes Ursula but we must make haste for as you know we have limited amount of time let us bestow our blessings on him before we dissipate."

Ursula stood on the left side of Merlin as she placed her hands in his heart as well as his head, Norwick did the same. Their hands filled with luminous light as they filled Merlin with their powers glowing red lights and green lights cursed through Merlin as Norwick and Ursula gave their power over the mind, foresight, Ursula gave her knowledge of the magi spells. Norwick imparted his strength with power over elements. Merlin was empowered with these gifts but when he fell through the time stream he lost his abilities. Norwich continued to give powers of transformation. Merlin eyes began to flutter his body shook and quivered when he received all the magi powers.

Merlin began to rise from his lifeless state his body flexed in all directions his muscles contorted as the swelled due to all the power he retained. Merlin arose revitalized as he exited the stone circles. He was reminded of Ursula and Norwick a sudden rush of warmth came over his body indicating that Ursula and Norwich were at peace. Merlin set off to set his retribution on the one who took his family away from him Desmoria.

Desmoria/Ezerbeth sensed Merlin presents it was time to take matter into her own hands for she was worried about her pact with Lucifer. Demoria/Ezerbeth considered,"**How could she corrupt Merlin?** She searched her mind trying to find the answer she delved deep into her mother's memories of Merlin. Demoria felt Mab's ultra-hatred for Merlin.

Mab loathed him in the womb as he fought and clawed to be first borne. She witnessed how Mab maneuvered her mother to take her to the underworld. Desmoria observed where Mab drew her powers of evil and darkness from the dammed souls in Hellfire. Desmoria viewed how Mab controlled Helfestis like a puppet that was until Merlin intervened and wiped her memory and bound her forever to be a vampire.

Mab never gave up her obsession to become all powerful. Even when the family set to Earth she murdered her own parents without blinking an eye Desmoria lavished in the pure evil of her mother. She learned that no matter what her trap Mab was never powerful enough to defeat Merlin.

Tormented with the facts Desmoria fell to utter despair as she contemplated further "How can I defeat him?" **Merlin all power immortal what is you weakness?** Merlin in all the memories of her mother Mab she always saw Merlin come to aid of his fellow man, Merlin cared for mortal he put his faith and love in humans. Merlin favored Solana he was crushed when she took her vows as Lady of the Lake his heart was broken. That is it that is how I will corrupt Merlin. I will use his love of humans to shift him to the dark side. I must seek the aid of Lucifer once more. I have to devise a way for Merlin to fall in love with me so I can bend him to my will. Once Merlin is in love with me he will do whatever I say then I will make him do unspeakable things to humans he loves so dear. Once that is done I will have paid my debt to Lucifer I will be free from my bond to hell. Then I will be able to put my plans into action as my mother before me I will rule as I lay siege to these mortals.

Desmoria hurried through the castle to the darkest recesses of her apothecary. The room was bolted shut with a magical lock. Demoria moved quickly as she moved her hand in upward in a circular motion and the spoke the spell of illumination as soon as she uttered the words sparks of fire lit the door face she placed her hand on her smoky purple amulet the fire dissipated as the amulet was centered in the middle of the door. The amulet glowed bright purple with pink rose hue Desmoria's fingernails grew outward into triangular points Desmoria place her triangular nails inside the door facing and turned the bright purple rose hued amulet as it turned the slots on both sides of the door unbolted and the door opened.

Solana was poised to find out as much as she could about the jewels of power but she did not want to let on to much about her true intentions. Helena, Uther, Pegasus, and Solana headed toward the North Sea where the Phoenix was being held prisoner.

The coast of the North Sea was not welcoming at all the sea raged against the land  deep inlets of rivers towering sheer cliffs surrounded them on either side as they headed down the massive mountain toward the raging sea gigantic waves crashed against the land as the black murky water covered the land with debris. Large whirlpools swirled around them. Choppy thrusting winds kept most away. Helena, Uther, Solana, and Pegasus would not be deterred from their course. Helena called upon the powers of the Earth as she placed her hands down into the hardened soil the earth quake Helena dug her hands deep within the soil forcing the Earth to move forward creating a bridge of land made of harden rock with tree roots emerged covering the large chasm over the North Sea.

Pegasus began to run leaping into the air. Pegasus stretched his wings outward to combat the massive winds as the air collided together it stopped the raging sea. Helena cried out,  "Solana now you must take hold of the sea you must open the whirlpool in the center so Uther has a pathway."

Helena called upon the powers of the forest to encompass Uther is a protective suite Helena looked deep within Uther's steel blue eyes as she spoke to his minds eyes and ordered him to enter the whirlpool seek out the Phoenix prison break the chains with Excalibur to free the Phoenix place Excalibur in her line of site and bring her to me. Uther walked on the bridge Solana stood in the center of the bridge as she called upon the powers of The Lady Of The Lake the half-moon on her forehead began to shine a radiant blue as her eyes turn backward into her head Solana arms moved forward in the direction of the whipping whirlpool water flowed from her eyes cleared a path for Uther.

Uther walked off the bridge and plunged into the murky depths of the swirling whirlpool. Solana held the path as Uther enter the center of the whirlpool. There was a dark metallic cube that was covered in chains. Uther raised Excalibur into the heaven as a powerful emerald beam burned through the sky to ignite Excalibur as the sapphire glowed with a blue tint in one fluid motion Uther struck down the sword and broke the chains with a loud thunderous explosion.

The whirlpool shut in on itself the course waters shot into the air knocking the bridge askew. Pegasus was thrown into the air as Solana held on grasping at what was left of the rock face bridge Excalibur broke the chains as the metallic cube started to shift as it fell deeper into the sea floor.

Uther dove after the cube in his protective suite he could breathe under the water. He caught up the cube and thrust Excalibur into the center of the cube. The metallic prisons cracked as it split apart to reveal a beautiful women encased in a circular ball of water. Uther could not believe his eyes flowing fire red hair soft supple tan skin curvaceous backside bountiful plump breasts Uther was overwhelmed with this breathtaking vision of the beauty that was before him. The phoenix eyes started to flutter as her weightless body moved gyrating she jerked against the water ball Uther knew he had to act fast to make sure the Phoenix would not drown. Uther burst the out of the water and shouted to Solana, "Burst the water bubble now."

Pegasus flew down and scooped Solana up onto his back Solana focused all her power on bursting the water bubble blue light came shooting out of her half-moon on her forehead a beam of blue light caused the water bubble to burst instantly as Uther and the Phoenix were inside the whirlpool Solana took the last bit of strength she had cause the north sea to shoot up a geyser that collected Uther and the Phoenix as they erupted out of the north sea to the sheer cliffs next to Helena.

The Phoenix was dazed for a moment as soon as she felt the warmth of the sunlight on her skin the picturesque vision of women transformed into an immense fierce bird like creature with wings made of fire the plumage of feathers started inward were of white heat orange to scale a ruby red to the out. The Phoenix was site to behold golden talons with and enormous beak sharp to the very touch I am free, I am free she shouted to the heavens the majestic bird hurled herself into the sky as she caught site of Pegasus. She changed her direction and flew over to his direction. "It cannot be as I live breath is it really you? What happened to us why were we imprisoned?"

Pegasus looked to his dear friend as he explained the betrayal of the gods how they imprisoned all the animals of war without a care. The Phoenix could not believe what she was hearing the tears streamed down her face. She let a shrieking cry that could be heard for miles making Uther, Helena, and Solana's ears bleed.

Solana was the first to hear her cry as she raised her hands to cover her ears she lost her grip on Pegasus and began to fall into the North Sea. Pegasus drove after her catching her in the nick of time. Uther was next to hear the awful howl from the Phoenix which sent him to his knees. Helena followed soon after. Pegasus flew with Solana on his back landed next to Helena and Uther. The Phoenix still in the air watched puzzled as to why Pegasus would help these mortals. They Phoenix followed Pegasus when she landed she transformed into her human form The Phoenix was astoundingly beautiful she has fiery red hair flowing in the wind soft supple tawny skin and emerald eyes. Helena called upon the trees to cloth the Phoenix with leaves from the forest.

The Phoenix reacted by setting the leaves ablaze I require no help with attire with a wave of her hand she clothed herself with vibrate golden and red feathered skin tight gown Phoenix walk toward Pegasus as she asked, "Why do you lend aid to these mortals?"

Pegasus counter, "Phoenix we are in a terrible world where humans rule the gods have turned their backs on us. Helena is the only survivor of the Hyperion age. She is all that remain of the tree creatures. It was the gods who imprisoned us these mortals are aiding us as we release all the animals of war. The Manicore and Leviathan are both still imprisoned once we rescue them we will set forth to Mt Olympus to exact our revenge on the gods for their betrayal." Uther stood motionless still in his trance Solana spoke up, "Phoenix all of us were wronged by the gods my name is Solana I was chosen against my will to be a vessel for the goddess. I never had a chance to follow my heart. The goddess pulled me away from my one true love and I will seek my vengeance.

Helena interjected, "I too was wronged by the gods as they siege to my people in a mass killing of the tree creatures. In one fall of Zeus's thunderbolt my people were set ablaze. I vowed that day to seek justice for my people. Uther is the only mortal here because he carries the sword of power Excalibur. It is made so only a mortal can wield the sword. Excalibur also holds a jewel of time Uther's sole is pure."

Pegasus looked to everyone as he addressed them, "We have no time to waste we must head to Sagimel Mountains where Leviathan is held captive deep in the white crest mountains the journey will be long and arduous so let us begin."

# CHAPTER FIVE
# DESMORIA'S SCHEME

Desmoria/Ezerbeth knew her only chance was to summon Lucifer to combat Merlin. She realized the time has come she must call upon the powers of the dark. She entered the apothecary it was pitch black Desmoria/Ezerbeth chanted the spell of illumination as the torches in the room began to light one by one.

The room was filled with horrors of body parts dangled from the ceiling, potions, and vials of ingredients. The room had an altar in the middle of the black triangle. The alter was made of grinded up bones from Desmoria/Ezerbeth victims. On the outside in the black triangle of sanctum at the three points held vials.

The first was filled with crow's blood, the next was filled with eyes of children, and the third was filled with serpents. Desmoria/Ezerbeth place the amulet of evil on the secret alter. She began to circle the triangle chanting the incantation, "I call upon the lord of the dark I call upon Lucifer head of Hades come to my aid I call upon the prince of darkness Lucifer come to me." Desmoria/Ezerbeth circled the triangle three times. On the third and last time the vials around the triangle exploded emulating red, black, and orange light beamed out of the ground. The amulet glowed a vibrant purple as black smoke filled the air Lucifer appeared and stood atop the alter.

"Why have you called upon me? Is our plot afoot to corrupt Merlin? Desmoria/Ezerbeth your time grows short soon you will join me in Hades forever." Desmoria/Ezerbeth bowed in Lucifer's presents, "Please dark lord I call upon you for my second of three favors." Lucifer walked around the alter taking his gifts.

Lucifer picked up the children's eyes and ate them slowly as he enjoyed every bite. He then moved on to the next broken vial to see the serpent trying to slither away. Lucifer bend down to pick it up with his hands. Lucifer moved the snake close to his mouth as he milked the sweet venom from the fangs of the serpent until it was lifeless in his hand. Lucifer devoured the snake as he tasted the savory flesh of the serpent his eyes widened with pleasure. Lucifer collected the crow's blood as it stood seeping into the floor of the triangle of sanctum Lucifer stuck out his forked tongue and sucked the crow's blood out of the floor drinking every last drop.

Lucifer content with his gifts answered, " Desmoria/Ezerbeth I will grant your request but be warned you will only have one favor left so make sure you asked wisely for you favor." Desmoria/Ezerbeth thought for a moment, "Lucifer I have thought long and hard about how to get Merlin to join us. Dark Lord the only weakness Merlin has is mortals. He feels for them and cares for their wellbeing. I would like to request that you provide me with a love spell to charm Merlin to toy with his heart. I believe if I get him to fall in love with me I will have power over him. Lucifer I must ask wisely as you said. So in addition to my request you must capture Merlin's one true love Solana. Lock her away for safe keeping. This will ensure I have the ability to control him if the love spell does not work. Lucifer Dark lord please placate my request."

Lucifer was intrigued by Desmoria/Ezerbeth request as he responded, "What you ask can be done at a price Desmoria you must give one of your children as a sacrifice I will be able to grant that request. Desmoria looked to Lucifer with confusion, "my child Lucifer as you know I am unable to have a child?" Lucifer answered back.

"You must sacrifice one of the males from your house Desmoria. She interjected, "Yes of course dark lord I have two upstairs which do you require?" Lucifer thought for a moment and retorted, "I require the first born. Without blinking an eye she countered, "Yes my lord right away."

Desmoria/Ezerbeth hurried out of the apothecary to the children's nursery Desmoria/Ezerbeth pick up the child from the warmth of his feathered bed. The child fast asleep became startled as Desmoria/Ezerbeth pick him up in her arms; the babe started to cry loudly as the castle began to stir. Desmoria/Ezerbeth knew she had to think fast in order to avoid being questioned as to why she had woken up the babe from his slumber. Desmoria/Ezerbeth knew the only way she could do this was to quite the child was to place her hand over the babe mouth. Desmoria/Ezerbeth levitated into the air holding the babe in her arms as the nurse maid came to see what the matter was.

The nurse deprived of sleep lazily walked into the nursery her eyes barely opened as she headed toward the crib. The nurse looked down to see only one babe in the cradle before she could think she rubbed her eyes to make sure she was not seeing things in a closer look still only one babe in the crib.

The nurse let out a blood curdling scream of terror. The knight guard rushed to the woman to see the horror for himself. The heir to the throne was gone snatch out of his bed. The knight rushed down the hall and the nurse grabbed the other babe and headed down to her room. Desmoria/Ezerbeth landed with the babe in her arms and hurried to the apothecary Desmoria/Ezerbeth presented the babe to Lucifer as instructed Desmoria/Ezerbeth placed the babe on the altar. The babe started to squirmed struggling arching his small body with all his might to no avail.

Lucifer took his long cloven hands as he reached to stoke the babe laying in the center of the alter once his rough black cloven hands touch the babe his skin burned. Lucifer lifted the babe into the air with one motion he tore the child in half as the babe life-force drained on the altar.

Lucifer placed his fingers in the pure blood of the child without sin as he swirled the blood around and around concentrating Solana the blood pooled on the alter started to smolder faster and faster Lucifer circled the blood with his finger as a small portal opened, in the portal Lucifer saw Solana on a hillside but what

was this Pegasus and the Phoenix it cannot be? Lucifer was confused this is a mistake there is no way?
Lucifer wasted no time he swirled the portal making it big enough for him to travel through. Lucifer jumped in to see Solana on the sea cliff. Lucifer had to act fast before she could see him.

Lucifer knew he had to be devious to fool The Lady of the Lake. Lucifer needed powerful magic to travel through the time stream as well as to deceive Solana Lucifer used a glamour spell to change his form. Lucifer transformed into Merlin. Solana was on her way to join the others in-route to Sagimel Mountains. It was if something told her to turn around as she saw a flash of white light that was followed by a huge explosion on the other side of the cliff.

Solana gasp awe stuck as she saw her beloved Merlin, Solana rushed to the edge of the cliff running towards Merlin. She was mesmerized as all her feeling of love bubbled to the surface all at once. Solana realized he was on the other side of this huge chasm Solana beckon Merlin to come to her.
Lucifer disguised as Merlin levitated over to her. Merlin is it true are you finally here with me? I cannot believe my eyes what happened to you? Where have you been all this time?"

 Lucifer had to act quickly before Solana became suspicious and his deceptive game would be over. He moved towards her without uttering a word which Solana found very odd.  He reached his arms to embrace her Lucifer's cloven hands brushed against her skin Lucifer's enchantment dispersed.

Solana eyes widened with fear as she looked upon the hideous creature Lucifer his red scaled skin with the gigantic black horns and cloven hands and feet his puncheon aroma of death and decay. Solana's face lost all it color as fear encompassed her. The beating of her heart raced as it leapt into her throat.

She tried to scream but she could not murmur a word Lucifer grabbed her with both hooves as Solana's body burned, Lucifer shouted, "Enough you come with me lady of the lake!" On pure instinct she struggled with all her might fighting against Lucifer.

Pegasus was the first to notice she was gone. Pegasus called out for Solana with no reply he circled back to the cliff face to see Solana in a struggle with none other than the fallen god himself Lucifer.

Pegasus came to a startling halt to see the fallen god in all his splendor. Pegasus began to reflect, **Lucifer was a beautiful god who had become prideful he has become jealous of his brother Zeus and his power. Lucifer tried to overthrow his brother by challenging Zeus.**

His brother was the most powerful god accepted to the challenge in exchange Lucifer demanded if he was victorious that he would be King of the gods forever .Zeus accepted the terms with one condition that if Zeus won Lucifer would be banished forever from Mt. Olympus cast down to the depths of mouth of hell never again to walk among his brothers and sisters. Lucifer agreed. Zeus battled with Lucifer in his arrogance he overlooked the fact the Zeus was all powerful no matter what attack he choose Zeus counter until he had his fill of sport. Zeus called a mighty thunderbolt down scaring Lucifer with a horrible deformity half god half bull his skin scorch and burn leaving scales of scarlet cloven hooves replaced where his once beautiful hands and feet were like a beast ebony horn grew out of each side of his massive head. A long skinny tail grew out of his backside. The final indignity was his mouth was engorged with a forklike tongue. Zeus open the clouds of Mt Olympus as he cast Lucifer down to the mouth of hell evermore.

Pegasus flew high above the clouds to conceal his presents as he watched Lucifer trying to abduct The Lady of the Lake. Solana struggling as rage and fear took over power started to grow as her eyes rolled in the back of her head her heart beat faster and faster he vein stood on end. The North Sea began to rage as the wind began to pick up causing the waters to swirl and grew stronger and more violent with each swell. Waves crashed against the rock face. Solana was entranced as her power took full effect. A tidal wave hurling toward the cliff face ensued. The massive wave collided with the land knocking Lucifer off his footing which sent him hurling into the rock face horns first.

Lucifer stuck with the rock face tried to maneuver out of his imprisonment. He was growing tired of trying to break free.

Frustrated he was sent into a mad rage. Embers of flames grew within his eyes focused on the fire within. Lucifer eyes started to burn sending out flames to soften the rock face just enough for him to break loose.

Lucifer took hold of Solana as she stood entranced he pointed down to the Earth where they stood and moved his cloven hoof in a circle as he thrust his hoof down the ground burrowing beneath them as he push further and further down the opening above was closing. Pegasus flying above watching as he waited. Plotting the best moment to take action. Lucifer was pushing ever deeper with the Earth. The opening was started to close as Pegasus flew into action charging down to the opening just making it in the nick of time. Pegasus knew he needed to keep the Earth from crashing in on itself forever blocking any way of escape. He flew down to the opening. He began to run in a circle making a path Pegasus used his feathers from his wings to hold circled opening from closing in on itself.

Solana and Lucifer reached the middle of the Earth where he encased her into a tomb of glass and steel. Solana did not put up a fight and fainted dead away inside her imprisonment. Lucifer pleased with himself achieving part of the favor for Desmoria/Ezerbeth smiled with sheepish grin as he deliberated his next phase of the favor, now *he must find a love spell that will be powerful enough to have Merlin the magi dragon wizard fall in love with Desmoria.*

The castle was in hysterics about the missing prince. The knight's guard searched every end of the castle to no avail. Desmoria/Ezerbeth crept into the hall as she made herself look as if she was awaken from her slumber. Everyone was running around in circles looking high and low for the prince.

Desmoria/Ezerbeth shouted, "WHAT IS THE MEANING OF THIS!!!" The ladies in waiting rushed to her side as they bowed in her presents the head lady in waiting murmured in a soft meek voice, "My Queen the prince is missing we have searched the castle high and low. Although Desmoria/Ezerbeth knew the fate of the babe she did not want to let on.

She cried out, "My son my precious boy who would do this? Who would rip a suckling babe from the bosom of its mother? Where is my dear son? Find him now call the guard at once. I want to speak to my advisor now. I want to know what vile enemies of the kingdom would sink this low. Well do not grovel hurry make haste."

 As the ladies waiting set to their duties Desmoria/Ezerbeth took the dismembered babe out into the courtyard as she threw the entrails and babes lifeless body in a nearby merchant dwelling. Desmoria/Ezerbeth knew full well that the merchants would wake with mourn sun. She knew they would discover the body. Desmoria/Ezerbeth headed back to the castle as she awaited the discovery of the murdered prince.

Tobish awoke like every other morn. Tobish was a humble man of meeker meaning he trades glassware and finery. Tobish arose to a minuscule break feast of uneven bread with some goat cheese and mead. He walked down the alley to his shop. Tobish shop was in the center of trade bazaar he entered the shop as he did every other day began to face all the shelves take stock then open the doors for trade. Tobish was taking stock when he noticed some of the jugs were out of place. Tobish found that very odd, *"Now how did this happen?"* he wondered. He bent down to straighten the jugs. Tobish on further investigation found bloody entrails of what he thought was an animal that had escaped a hunter. Tobish followed the trail of blood to find a small baby hand and severed head lay at his feet. The babe was dressed in royal bed clothes.

 Tobish knew the moment he saw the kingdoms seal that it was the prince. The sweet innocent soul was brutally torn in two in a malicious act of sure violence. Tobish was beside himself at the sure thought of the horror that had befallen the poor prince.

Tobish grew fearful for he was just mere merchant who would have to deliver this horrible news to the Queen. This would kill her with the passing of the King just last year. Tobish thought, **how can I a mere merchant tell our beloved queen about this horrific death of her dear prince**. Tobish knew it was his duty but he still feared the queen's reaction.
The Queen called for her advisor to find out the enemies of the Kingdom. The advisor was an elderly man tall and lanky. The advisor approached the queen, "You called my grace how may I

be of service?" She retorted, "I must know our enemies the prince has been abducted from his bed tell me who would do this?" The advisor contemplated for a moment as he replied, "Well your grace there are only two that spring to mind Lord Baraha and King Crue my queen. Each have intent on the throne as well as both border our kingdom not to mention that both are in line to the throne should something happen to the prince."

The queen was stunned to hear news that others conspired against her Kingdom, "I order you to send the knights to each land in search of the prince bring me back my son or bring me their heads on a pike." The advisor bowed as he answered, "Yes my Queen" the advisor left Desmoria/Ezerbeth as he sent the orders to the knight.

The queen addressed the court fears instilling hope that all would return to normal. The queen retired to her quarters. She lay in her quarters awaiting her chance to go back to apothecary. Desmoria/Ezerbeth siege her opportunity when the ladies in waiting headed on to their respective duties.

No sooner than she had arrived in the apothecary that Lucifer appeared with the love spell Desmoria eyed Lucifer like he was mutton dinner with all the trimmings. As he held her future in his hands. Lucifer held a vial of pinkish purple liquid that was bubbling the aroma was awful the smell of rotting meat.

"Here is your love spell you must lure Merlin here when the moon is full at the height of the witching hour he must drink the entire potion once he has drank the entire potion you must look directly into his eyes and kiss him. Merlin will be mesmerized by you."

Desmoria filled with delight at the thought of Merlin at her beckon call. She knew she had to work fast she must message Merlin to get him to castle at the right time. Desmoria would have to exhaust her power to focus on Merlin's mind's eye luring him to the castle. Desmoria set he plan into action.

The castle guard went in search of the missing prince. Tobish let out a terrifying scream that sent guards into a screeching halt. The guard approached his shop with caution sword at the ready, "What goes on speak up!" the lead guard shouted. "Please sir I am a humble merchant I opened my shop to this horrific sight my lord."

The lead guard crept into the shop as he enter the guard saw the horrors awe stricken he rushed out of the shop and vomited on the side of the shop. Tobish bowed and looked to the ground as the guard finished his disgrace. "You come with me the queen must know of this and all details."

The guard took Tobish on this horse and rushed back to the castle He instructed the other two guard to wrap the body and bring him back to the castle. The two guards took the castle banner down and used it to wrap the lifeless prince gently into the banner as they proceeded to the castle.

Desmoria/Ezerbeth could sense that guards coming back and returned to her quarters. She lay in her bed looking grief stricken over the prince's abduction. Tobish and the lead guard rushed through the castle to the throne room the court was assembled activities were solemn as everyone was in despair.

The lead guard approached on baited breath as he looked to the ladies in waiting," I must see the queen immediately hurry and fetch her." The ladies scurried to the queen's quarters where she lay sleeping. Valeria head of the ladies approached the bed chamber to arouse the queen she whispered in the queens ear, "My queen you have been requested in the throne room please awaken."
The queen tossed and turned as began to awaken she rubber her tear stained eyes as she yawned slightly. "Who has request me do not understand I am overwrought with worry about the prince." Valeria interjected my queen it is the lead guard who has requested you presents I believe it is in regards to the prince's disappearance."
The queen arose, "Well what are we waiting for let us hurry." The queen dressed quickly and headed to the throne room. The queen entered to see the court bow as she sat upon the throne. "Well what news have you speak up?" The queen demanded. The lead guard shoved Tobish in front of the queen. Tobish was a bundle of nerves as shiver ran down his spine with all the strength he could muster on trembling voice he cried out, "My queen it is with great regret that I have grave news about the prince." The queen's eyes widen as she heard the words, "What does he mean?" As she look to the lead guard. He interjected, "Your

majesty the dear prince was found. It is with heartfelt sadness I must tell you that your beloved son was brutally murdered in the courtyard this very morn. Tobish of the merchant guild found your babe scattered among his shop." Tobish bow to the ground daring not to look upon the queen awaiting her reaction. The Queen gasp as she cired out, "WHY! Not my babe not the dear sweet prince it is not true. How could this happen? To take a babe from his mother an innocent child?"

The queen began to sob uncontrollable as Valeria dismissed the court. "What did you see shop keeper, speak up." The queen demanded. Tobish told what he witnessed to the queen. The queen wanted to see her son "Take me to the prince chamber." The queen looked upon the lifeless body of the prince as he lay torn to shreds across his cradle. The queen rushed to his side as she sobbed she cursed her enemies as well as the gods for letting this happen.

Desmoria/Ezerbeth laid it on thick so she would not lose face in front of the court or the kingdom it was a beautiful performance everyone was fooled the queen excused herself to her quarters too distraught to press on.

# CHAPTER SIX
# MERLIN'S ASSAULT

Merlin was rejuvenated as he set his sights on avenging his family. He would put an end to Desmoria's reign of terror once and for all. Merlin was fixated on her every move. As he sat in wait he watched her actions over the past few years. Merlin witnessed how she placed herself in position as queen.

Desmoria married a brutal savage man who was evil down to the core. Merlin had never seen a person with such a sadistic nature like the Duke. His lust for power even out shadowed his own sister Mab. The duke would raid the outlining lands taking everything in his path nothing was overlooked.

He would torment any he took prisoner in vile ways. He took the innocents of women on whim when he fancied carnal pleasures. The Duke was also known to defile animals as well. Once he humiliated them as if it were not enough. He would slaughter them in cold blood as he ate their flesh raw. The duke held nothing back in the marriage bed with his vile demonic sexual acts of pleasure and pain taking his queen at any time that suited.

Desmoria herself never suffered one indignity as she procured a peasant to endure the Dukes sexual horrors. The duke would complete his horrific acts as he drifted off to slumber Desmoria would take the peasants to the dungeon. She sustained them until they birth a babe.

Desmoria ripped the babe from mother's arms. The mother would then become feast for Desmoria as she would gorge herself on the mother's flesh and afterbirth of the child. She did this to establish the mother's bond with her child. Desmoria would hang the peasants upside down and drain them of any remaining blood. She was successful in her charade.

She was growing tired of the duke so she devised a plan to have him killed. She hired a mercenary to violently kill the duke and any that stood in her way to the throne.

As a women she could not ascend to the throne Desmoria was a cunning minx she had her first born accept his birthright as king. Desmoria knew that she would serve as regent until the babe was of age to take the throne. Merlin watched everything unfold as he learned about his enemy her ruthless nature. Her immeasurable lust for power, and her insatiable hunger was taking over

Merlin continued to fixate on her as she would go out combing the streets for eager ladies and men who wanted to boost their station. How she preyed on the weak using mortals as a food supply as easily as Merlin would eat a piece of fruit.

Desmoria would discard and drain peasants of their life-force. Merlin continued to see her wreak havoc on the people as well as the land were suffering in her wake. Merlin had seen enough it was time to take action. Merlin gathered all of his enchantments the ruby dagger, the emerald necklace of the vampires, and Norwick spell book. Merlin transported himself back to the Carpathian Mountains ready to wage war to end Desmoria once and for all.

The clever minx herself was plotting a trap for Merlin to come face to face. Desmoria built her defenses up increased the power of her force field as well as made sure that her apothecary was fully protected where her food supply was store.

The kingdom itself was turmoil over the sudden death of the baby prince. Desmoria degreed that the court and servants leave the castle. The queen was overcome with grief at the loss of her son. She could not bear to walk the hallowed halls as she mourned. The queen was after all Desmoria in disguise. She wanted everyone gone so she could unleash her enslavement of Merlin not because she was grieving.

All the nobles and servants vacated the castle. Now she was alone Desmoria looked over all her books for spells to make sure that if the love potion did not work she had another spell to hold Merlin. Desmoria wanted to make sure she would not endure the wrath of Merlin. She ventured out of the castle to the forest. She went to seek out an occult priest.

Desmoria search the wooded forest deep within thick underbrush spread between the trees, not a beam of sunlight slips through the forest branches. Only when the sun sets, can one see its glory. The bark of the trees are a chestnut brown, the leaves are an evergreen. As she headed ever closer to the occult priest lair the beauty of the forest dwindled as a murky gloom began to ooze forward.

The trees leaves changed from the vibrant green to a decaying dark brown. The bark on the trees turn to rot. A gloomy fog like mist filled the air as Desmoria spotted off in the distance a small cavern. She headed toward the cavern the rot and decay seemed to grow worse the closer she got to the cavern dead toadstool, fungus, spiders, even the soil itself turns into a kind of black sludge. The occult priest was inside the cavern working on his spells when he heard off in the distance a stranger approaching.

 The occult priest was a small dwarf man who was badly scared from burns he suffered as a child when his family tried to burn him to death because they though he was an abomination to the gods. The man smelled of death, he had beady green eyes and his back was humped over.

The occult priest moved toward the cavern entrance as he watch Desmoria headed in his direction. He stood outside the cavern as he shouted to Desmoria, "Why have you come here?" Desmoria saw the small dwarf,
"I seek your aid occult priest. I am in need of a binding spell to trap a powerful necromancer. "

The occult priest was intrigued by this women's remark, "Who is this powerful necromancers you speak of women." Desmoria knew she must let on her true intentions to this occult priest because although she was powerful she knew that his power surpassed hers. If she were to give away her plan the occult priest could usurp her efforts and take this land for himself.
  "I wish to charm a lover occult priest. I misspoke I meant a romancer not necromancer he has wronged me and I want to make him pay will you help me."   The occult priest grinned as he spoke, "Oh I see I will aid in your deception but you must meet my price"

  Desmoria was not going to enter into any bargain without knowing the terms.  "Well what is it that you require as payment priest." The occults priest beady green eyes flashed with delight as he told Desmoria his terms "I require scales of a sea serpent, the tail of dragon, the wings of a fairy and a lock of hair from the goddess as payment."
Desmoria was enthralled, "you are mad how am I to get suck things I am only a simple woman after all. The occult priest looked to Desmoria as he eyes looked her up and down, "my lady you may fool others with your veil of disguise but I know your true identity, Desmoria of old."

"Dam you priest if you knew my linage what makes you believe I can acquire suck things."  The occult priest nodded, "You are not just Desmoria of old you are Lucifer spawn all powerful vampire she devil.  If you cannot acquire these things who can?"

Desmoria frustrated, "Fine I will provide you with your items but I have little time so I must be transported to each location post haste. I also need the sacred dagger of the ancients in the old world." The occult priest was in shock he was under the impression that Desmoria had the ruby dagger, "You mean you don't have the ruby dagger?" Desmoria growing more and more frustrated began to shout, "That dagger is the only thing that will penetrate a dragon's flesh or sever fairies wings. If you want these items you must have the ruby dagger. Do you not have it Desmoria after all you killed the magi dragon with it?" Desmoria sighed, "No I thrust the dagger into the beast and fled because I feared Merlin. The occult priest was shocked, "WHAT come again what could possibly scare you."

"Have you not heard of Merlin in your wisdom the magi dragon Merlin? Wizard of Koldacot the supreme power of Avalon. The occult priest eyes widens as Desmoria spoke of Merlin, "You don't mean Melkar the all-powerful do you? He is known throughout the land his power rivals that of the gods themselves tell me you do not mean him."

Desmoria looked to him in astonishment, "Yes one in the same I killed his grandfather I was born of his sister Mab ending the line." The occult priest began to pass back and forth with worry as Desmoria finished "Melkar is going to seek his vengeance upon you in order to bind such a necromancer that is the price I require.
Desmoria had no choice she must gather all the things and fast she waved her hands as she was transported to the Baltic Sea. She

called to Poseidon god of the sea. Poseidon was the son of Cronus, god of earth, and his wife, Rhea.

Cronus overthrew his father's rule by fatally wounding him. The dying father prophesied that Cronus would likewise be overthrown by one of his own children. As a result, upon the birth of each of his children, Cronus had eaten each of his children imprisoning them in bowels of his entrails. The offspring he had eaten were Hestia, Hades, Zeus, Poseidon, Hera and Demeter. As the children grew in the bowels of their father's entrails they devised a plan of escape.

Hades, Zeus, and Poseidon pooled their powers and escaped their imprisonment. Once they took over Mt. Olympus Poseidon, Zeus and their brother Hades cast lots to equally divide regions of the world for themselves. Poseidon acquired the sea with Zeus claiming the heavens, Hades taking the underworld and earth as neutral ground. Poseidon established rule of the sea from the underwater realm of Aegae, named for a mortal city sacred to him. He rarely traveled to Olympus. Desmoria had to summon the powerful Poseidon. The tides was coming on the shore now was the time as she chanted the spell to invoke the powerful sea god.

 Desmoria cried out, "Poseidon, god of the sea I pray to thee in earnest to aid me
in this hour, your need is dreariest Almighty you are, yes indeed. With powers of the ocean at your command you are the master of

the sea. I pray the grace of your blessing,
to aid me. So mote it be! Long live Poseidon, the god of the sea!

As soon as the last word was spoken deep in the center of the Aegae arose a massive sea weed shaped crown began to drift to the surface of the sea a billowing silver three pronged trident soared out of the sea and there stood a colossal fishlike man riding on a whirlpool "Who dare call upon me?" He bellowed. Desmoria stood levitation above the sea I Desmoria who has called upon you Poseidon I seek your aid Poseidon looked up to the sky to see this little woman floating in the air, Poseidon began to laugh, "You request my aid a mere woman I will not yield to a silly levitating witch like you."

Poseidon moved his mighty trident into the air as he drew the winds to throw Desmoria into the nearby cliff. Desmoria held her ground she would not be moved. Poseidon was stunned to see this but he did not falter he held up his trident as he plunged it down deep into the sea. A tidal wave emerged with one quick motion of his hand he sent the huge wave in Desmoria's direction, "Now that should get rid of this pest."

Desmoria placed her hands out and the raging tidal wave was calmed. Poseidon knew he was not dealing with just mere mortal anymore. "Enough I need your aid Poseidon I will ask you one more time if you counter me this time I will be forced to release my full power upon you, now will you help me?" Poseidon knew when he was beaten and he gave in to Desmoria. Defeated he sighed, "Yes what do you require of me." Desmoria smiled as she told Poseidon that she need the scales of the titian sea serpent. "I will grant your request"

Poseidon dove into the dark depth of the sea where the titian was held. He took his massive trident and cut off the scales of the enormous sea serpent. With scales in hand he floated back to the surface and gave the shimmering scales to Desmoria.

Desmoria thanked Poseidon for his aid and jettison to her next task. Desmoria headed high above the cloud soaring to Mt. Olympus to gather the next thing a lock of hair from the goddess.

Merlin was on his way to the castle when his heart began to race he was given a horrible vision. Solana appeared in his mind's eye. Merlin witnessed Lucifer trick her into believing he has returned and in her moment of weakness Lucifer grabbed a hold of her and took her down the underworld. Merlin was enraged by the evil of the gods. **How could he let the lady of lake succumb to such horror? Where was the goddess to protect her?** Merlin thought to himself. Merlin transformed in a dragon and flew in the skies for Mt. Olympus. Merlin flew hard and fast to the god's home.

 Mt Olympus was formed after the gods defeated the Titans in the Titan War, and soon the place was inhabited by the gods. The Twelve gods lived in the gorges. Each god built their own palace. The pantheon was where they gathered together to consume nectar and ambrosia the substances which reinforces their immortality and discuss plans for the mortals.

The Throne of Zeus was made out of yellow marble that had small pieces of gold built into it for decoration. The throne was so large that it had seven steps leading up to it, each one colored with a color of the rainbow. There was a large blue covering over the throne, symbolizing the sky. On the right arm of the throne was a ruby-eyed eagle that had jagged strips of tin in its beak which symbolized that Zeus could kill any enemies by throwing lightning at them. Because the chair was made of marble, it was naturally cold. So Zeus had a purple ram's fleece over the chair. Zeus could shake this fleece over the world to create rain. The leader of the gods. From there he unleashed his thunderbolts, expressing his godly wrath.

It was like Avalon as well it had a barrier between the worlds. Merlin as a man could not enter the sacred land, Mt. Olympus. Merlin began to draw fire from within his throat. The heat surging through his nostrils smoke billowed out for either side as he emoted a huge fireball open the barrier. He was greeted by Zeus. The lord of the gods sat high upon his throne as he began to speak the ground shook, "Come closer Merlin I have been expecting you."

Merlin was a miniature lizard in Zeus's eyes. Merlin still enraged shouted, "How could you let Lucifer take The Lady of the Lake hostage? Why did the goddess not protect her?" Zeus became infuriated as he looked to Merlin, "I am Zeus Lord of the gods how dare you come here and insult me! Merlin your dear Solana had turned her back on the goddess as well as her service. She was consorting with Helena and the animals of war to overthrow the gods, Merlin. She wants to seek revenge on us for our betrayal. What would you have me do condone that behavior aid them in our destruction?"

Merlin was puzzled, "What do you mean she turned her back on her service?" Zeus threw his hands up in the air with frustration, "Oh I will tell you Solana was devastated when you left she prayed to the goddess for help the goddess refused so in turn Solana denounced the goddess. The goddess would not allow such desecration so she flawed Solana's beauty forever. Solana set her sights on a way to find you Merlin. She found an old script telling her how to open the portal through the era's with the jewels of time so she could be reunited with her beloved." Merlin was shocked to find out the Solana loved him after all this she was willing to risk everything just to be at his side once again. Merlin was truly humbled by this as he spoke up, "Here I am seeking vengeance I was blinded to Solana and her love for me I wanted to lash out and make that vile bitch Desmoria pay for destroying my family how could I be so wrong?"

Zeus understood his plight nodding in agreement, "Merlin you know no matter how much pain you inflict on Desmoria it will never heal that hole within yourself. She is immortal she will not die. Merlin, Desmoria made a pact with my brother if she does not fulfill her obligations she will be doomed to the depths of hellfire forever. Merlin you must return to your true course cast aside this vengeance."

Merlin knew the words he spoke were true as he nodded in accord, "How can I return Zeus? The portal of time was closed when I entered here." Zeus raised his hand outward circled it three times as a small portal opened Merlin saw Avalon on the horizon. He looked to Zeus with adoration as he entered the portal.

Merlin in the time stream knew he might loss his powers but it would be worth it for a chance to be with his love Solana again. Merlin looked in time as he walked everything moved backward before his eyes he watch the stream of time unravel as he stepped foot on the shores of Avalon once more.

This Avalon was changed it was deserted the lush green meadows with fragrant flowers were gone the streaming pools and waterfalls were gloomy. Merlin moved the veil between worlds to see the once pristine ivory castle. Merlin was surrounded by nothingness.

Merlin headed to the sanctuary where the priest and priestess were in abundance it was abandon. The land itself was devoid dying all around him, Merlin knew he must go in search of Solana before it was too late. Merlin thrust into the air above Avalon he searched the landscape to find more horrors once a green vibrate valley with lush hillsides were no more in its wake were dried fields failing forest even the rivers and lakes were dried up.

Merlin headed to the sea where Solana was abducted as he approached he found he was not alone in the skies. Merlin saw in the corner of his eye a flash of fire. Merlin spun around into a barrel roll as he moved into evasive maneuvers. The Phoenix had only seen a dragon once in her lifetime. She knew the beast was skillful in the art of war the Hyde of a dragon was impenetrable to every weapon.

The Phoenix alone would not be able to defeat such a powerful enemy. She decided it was best to stay her course as she flew off in the other direction. Merlin had never laid eyes on a more beautiful creature than the Phoenix those angelic wings of fire, her golden plum, large talons, and ruby eyes.
Merlin didn't know what to do because the Phoenix stood ground and did not attack he could not decipher if she was friend or foe. Merlin did sense she was afraid. Merlin could sense Solana before he had time to think his instincts took over as he transformed into his mortal self.

The Phoenix stood watching as this massive dragon turned to a mortal before her eyes. Now she could attack. She leaped into action she began to fly down claws first to tear Merlin limb from limb. She shot her nails from her talons large sharp knives of flames went racing towards Merlin.

 Merlin reacted immediately as he hear the fiery daggers whistle through the air. Merlin call upon the sea as he sent a wave of water splashing out the flamed nails deflecting them to the ground. The Phoenix was stunned to see her attack was so easily

counter never had she seen a mortal man have those abilities. The Phoenix decided to retreat before he sent his reprisal attack on her.
The Phoenix fled to a cavern as she transformed into her human form. Helena and Uther were looking for Pegasus. Merlin approached Helena, "Where is Solana, Helena? What is going on here? What is that in the sky? What has happened in my absence?"

Helena was bewildered to see Merlin but something about him was different somehow. It was as if he had aged overnight. In front of her stood a not a mere boy as she remembered but a man. Merlin's face was wore and wrinkled his blond lock now were grey.

"It is really you Merlin praise the gods you've returned. The land is in turmoil Merlin longtime friendships have ended the few kingdoms that remain are raging against one another fighting for supreme power. The land and the people are suffering. Merlin the goddess in a fit of rage struck down the tree creature in a murderous act."

Merlin did not care for the trouble of world he only care about Solana. Merlin exclaimed, "What of Solana tell me of my beloved Helena?" Helena looked to Merlin ashamed about what she was about to tell him, "That is the saddest tale of all. After you disappeared she became so inverted and depressed trying every way she could to find you. Solana turned her back on the goddess and Avalon. In doing so she was mutilated by the goddess. She joined us in our quest but she was tragically taken. We were in search of her when you appeared.

The Phoenix stayed back and listened as Helena was speaking to Merlin. "These demi gods conspire together I must warn Pegasus about this before it is too late." The Phoenix could speak to Pegasus through telepathy so she focused her mind as she relayed her message to Pegasus. Pegasus could not believe what he just witnessed as he pondered **Why Lucifer take Solana? What did he want her for? What part does she play in this? Why is she so important?**

Solana was placed in the dark surrounded by an unbreakable barrier. Solana exhausted her power trying to break free of her prison. Overcome with defeat she gave up curling herself into a ball crying out of pure despair to her circumstances.

Pegasus leaped to attention as the Phoenix message reached him. "We cannot trust these mortals. Helena is conspiring against us with someone named Merlin he is a powerful force as was demonstrated to me moments ago when he thwarted my attack. I don't know of his loyalty to the gods what should I do?" Pegasus responded back, "Wait Phoenix before you make a move if this person is who I think it is time to persuade him to our level of thinking."

Pegasus hurried back to Helena and the others. Merlin was astonished to see Pegasus. The magnificent sight of this massive winged horned horse. Pegasus bowed before Merlin. He was perplexed and did not utter a word.

Pegasus interjected, "I am Pegasus one of the animals of war that has suffered at the hand of the gods betrayed by our creator and imprisoned for these many years. Merlin all we seek is our chance to live our chance for justice. Merlin I implore you to aid in our quest to set my family free. Help us to seek our justice on Mt Olympus for their treachery. Please Merlin the gods have done nothing but damage this world with their constant interference I just tried to stop Lucifer from abducting The Lady of the Lake. Solana and I were unable to prevent it because I am limited in my power. I know where she is I can take you there now."

Merlin was puzzled to hear all of what Pegasus was saying but those thoughts vanished from his memory when he heard Solana's name, "Yes take me there now we have no time to lose" Merlin jumped on Pegasus back as they headed to the sight of Solana's abduction.

# CHAPTER SEVEN
# GAWAIN'S ARMY

Gawain has taken over the throne to the south. He had built his forces up to ensure he was ready for any rival kingdom attack. Gawain was a man of action he had grown confident in his new status as King Gawain.

But, he longed for adventure he wanted to prove his worth as King. He became disheartened when he learned that Garlois and Ingrien were wed without so much of an invitation sent to him.

Tarnish also set up his kingdom to the West. Tarnish as well built up his defenses from the able bodied men. He taught them the art of war, the skill of the lance, and the grace of the bow.

Tarnish too was not invited to Ingrien and Garlois recent nuptials he felt insulted. Tarnish sent for his royal page to relay a message to Gawain about his outrage at Ingrien and Garlois for their insult to him and his kingdom. He also express that he would like to visit Gawain's kingdom. The page wrote the message as he set off to the Gawain's kingdom in the South. The page rode all night to reach Gawain's castle with message in hand as he approached the castle gate.

The guards were just outside the gate meeting all visitors to ensure their intentions were noble. The page approached the guards and told them of his message for the king. The guards escorted the page through the massive halls of the castle to the king's chambers.

Gawain stood looking over his agenda for the day with his advisor when the guard approached. "Your highness this page comes with message from Tarnish king of the West do you wish to receive the message?"
Gawain was delighted to hear from his longtime friend Tarnish as he interjected, "Yes send him to me at once."

The page bowed in front of the king and handed him the message. Gawain read the message with glee he slapped the page on the back. "Boy tell your master he is welcome anytime he wishes to visit and relay I too was insulted at the folly of Garlois and Ingrien. Now be off with you boy."

The page left and soon arrived back to Tarnish with the message from Gawain. Tarnish set off for Gawain's kingdom. He arrived as he approached the head guard and asked for audience with the king. The guards knew of his arrival as they escorted him into the great hall with the court. He was greeted by the lords and ladies of the court as he was announced by the royal page.

Tarnish waited for Gawain as the king entered the great hall all the court bowed to him as he walked the procession of Earls, Dukes, Lords, and Counts were line to the right of him as the maidens, duchesses, ladies, and countess were to his left. Tarnish was to the head of the procession nearest to the throne. As soon as Tarnish landed eyes on his longtime friend he became overjoyed to see his robust companion in his finery Tarnish bowed to Gawain's feet as Gawain reach his massive hand down to his friend

"There is not a need for my brother in arms to bow to me come Tarnish let me see you." Tarnish stood in awe of his giant friend as he look him up and down "I see nothing has change my friend you are in the best of health." Tarnish replied, "I see you are in good form your highness." The two men embraced Tarnish expressed, "King Gawain my dear friend I wanted to speak with you in private if you would allow me an audience."

Gawain with a wry grin on his face exclaimed, "Yes of course Tarnish there is something I want to discuss with you as well come let us retire to more desired quarters where we can discuss these matters."

Tarnish and Gawain left the court and headed to the Kings chambers. Tarnish paced up and down trying to racking his brain on how to express his disgust about not being invited to the wedding of Garlois and Ingrien. As he was thinking of a clever way to broach the subject Gawain spoke up, "Tarnish it has come my attention that Uther was invited to Garlois and Ingrien wedding. I was also told that Solana was present as well. Tarnish I feel they have done my kingdom and yours a grave injustice like we unworthy to be part of their nuptials. I am highly offended and I am half out of my mind to make them pay for their arrogance in blood what about you good friend? "

Tarnish too was insulted but he did not think that was a reason to wage war. Gawain was thinking like a knight and not a king. Tarnish answered back, "I feel if we were taken seriously as a kingdom that they would not have overlooked us. Gawain growing more enraged as he came back with, "THAT speaks volumes for me!" Tarnish tried to calm Gawain as he countered, " I think we should make our presence known and our dislike expressed I feel an all-out war is a little drastic but still we should move forward with action."

Gawain understood his temper was getting the better of him as he exclaimed, "I am not a diplomat I want them to pay for their insolence. It is time to show our worth as kingdoms that will not be ignored. Tarnish saw his friend was very passionate about his kingdom as he interjected, "Yes I agree but are both our kingdoms ready?"

Gawain looked to Tarnish with bewilderment, "I have raised an army ready for battle in these few months. I am ready I ensure you. Tarnish what about you don't you too have forces?"

Tarnish did indeed have forces. Tarnish was not however sure of their abilities when it came to battle as of yet. As Gawain utter the last of his sentence Tarnish was struck with an idea. Tarnish turned to look at his friend with a devilish look in his eyes and a wide grin about his face as he retorted, "Wait Gawain this is perfect."

Gawain again looked puzzled, "What is perfect?"  Tarnish with amusements in his voice chuckled, "What if we invite Uther and Garlois here to compete in a tournament. We could wage their kingdoms forces. We would see firsthand the strengths and weakness as we use that to our own advantage. I believe that is the best course of action to take what say you Gawain."

Gawain thought to himself for a few moment before he answered back, "I believe you are right in this Tarnish we will get to see Uther and Garlois's armies in action as well as seek satisfaction for their insult."

Gawain called for his page, "Fetch my scribe boy and be quick about it."
The scribe entered the room with parchment and quill in hand. "Scribe invite then kingdoms to the north and east to our tourney as guest to compete in the games to prove your kingdoms worth bring your finest swordsmen, archers, and knights to castle Gawain a fortnight hence.  Now page ride with guards and deliver these messages to King Garlois and King Uther.

Tarnish left the king's chamber and scouted the grounds of castle Gawain. The great hall, the throne room, the massive courtyard and gardens the training arena where the knights trained as they mastered their skills and retired to their quarters. Tarnish thought about Gawain's comments about his forces.  **Are they up to the** task? **Were they ready for battle?** Tarnish's kingdom suffered the most losses after the skirmish with Mab. His kingdom was made up of farmers and minstrels.

Tarnish gathered all able bodied men in the land. He trained them in the skills of battle and warfare to defend their lands at any cost. Tarnish had little doubt about their abilities until this moment when Gawain asked him if his forces were ready for battle.

Now there was doubt creeping into his head about his knights. **Would they be ready? Although considering the time and the amount of training did Gawain's knights fare any better really? Better but still would Garlois or Uther's knights be in better condition?**


Gawain was so excited about the chance to prove his kingdom's worth. He raced to the knight's quarters and told them of the upcoming tourney. Gawain left it to the men to decide who should represent them in the games. He told the men when they decided to send the knights to meet him in the training arena. The men were overjoyed at the chance to prove their worth to their king and the other kingdoms.

The men knew each other's strengths and weakness so it was hard to select from the pool of knights so each knight drew lots. The four knights were chosen as they headed to the training field. Gawain awaited on the field as the men approached. He lead an all-out attack his sword raised at the ready shield up as the call to the archers were sounded flaming arrows whizzed by the men caught off guard. Gawain thrust his sword at them. The knight went on the defensive racing for cover they ran to a nearby log and hunkered down as they hid from flying arrows and a mad sword wielding king they search the area for better position Gawain shouted, "TAKE ARMS MEN, show me you are worthy to defend our kingdom!!" The men moved their position and headed toward the armory they grabbed their swords and shields as they struck back at Gawain who stood unmoved. The king called out and their fellow knights came onto the field archers at the ready fire. The arrows zoomed through the air as the swordsmen started a fierce attack on their fellow knights.

The four chosen knights thrust their swords in the fray. As the swords clashed sparks of amber filled the night sky as the four knights battled for their honor and their lives. Gawain watched from afar with conviction as they defended and overcame. He grew satisfied in knowing his kingdom was ready for anything that arose.

Gawain was confident about the men Gawain bellowed, "Enough you have proven your skill men retire to your quarters." The knight adjourned their training arena retiring to their quarters. Gawain looked for Tarnish as he searched the castle he could not find his companion anywhere. Gawain called for his page, "Where is King Tarnish?" The page replied, "sir he has retired to his chambers." Gawain who was also wary from his day decided to retire to his quarters as well.

Garlois awoke only to find the castle in an uproar as the court was scurrying around Garlois cried out, "WHAT is the matter?" Ingrien's lady in waiting answered back, "It is the queen my lord she is ill with fever many fear it's the work of the gods for not laying with you after you were wed Sir. I have been up all night with her majesty she has asked for the barber because she has been heaving all night.

Garlios raced to his wife side Ingrien was pale her body ached. She was so hungry but could not eat. She longed for sleep but remained awake. Garlois gently held Ingrien's hand as he stoked her forehead, "Ingrien my love what is the matter?" Ingrien lay there muttering to Garlois,
"I am afraid I have angered the gods by not allowing you to bed me on our wedding night." Garlois was overcome as he watched his beloved Ingrien suffering his heart sank deep in his chest. The barber arrived as he looked Ingrien over. He placed his hand on her head. The barber order the servant girl to fetch him some cold water. The barber continued to examine Ingrien. He held her throat as he felt of it. The barber then felt her belly.

The barber took King Garlois aside, "King joyful news are the tidings I bring for Queen Ingrien is with child." Garlois was elated at the news. "King Garlois heed my warning she must stay in bed for a while feed her only bland food unleven bread and soft vegetables.

Garlois looked to the barber and the ladies in waiting as he instructed them to not breathe a word of this news to the court. He wanted to be the one to announce when the time was right. Garlois left Ingrien's bed chamber as he headed to the throne room before he had reached the throne room he was met by one of the guards, "sir there is a messenger here from Glasgow kingdom requiring your audience." Garlois looked to the guard with puzzlement, "What are you going on about man? Who is the king of Glasgow?"

"My lord the king of Glasgow is Gawain." "WELL send him in so I can see what he wants right away," The messenger entered the great hall with the beautiful tapestry the large main hall was filled with wild flowers. He moved towards the throne room where the king sat upon a grand throne made of Ivory to each side of the throne were banners of Poseidon Trident echoed in silver with gold outlay.

The messenger approach the mighty throne he bowed, with his mighty voice he bellowed, "Garlois good king of the lands of the sea. My king Gawain send good tidings to you and your queen. King Gawain would like to invite you and your men to our tourney games to celebrate your recent nuptials to Lady Ingrien." Garlois found the request odd for Gawain was not present at his wedding but at any rate he thought it was a good chance to see how his knights would fare against the other kingdoms. Garlois motioned to the messenger, "Boy tell your master I accept and will compete in his games."

The messenger that headed north to Uther's Kingdom did not manage as well. When the messenger arrived he was meant with the grave news about King Uther. The messenger learned from King Uther's court that he disappeared right after his succession to the throne. "You see King Uther went in search of some wild game for the celebration feast. The weather had taken a turn for the worse so King Uther sought shelter for the night. It was rumored he was bewitched by the goddess. No one has seen the king since. Now as we speak our knights are out in search of our king."

The messenger was in shock he could not believe what he was hearing, "I must hurry back to tell King Gawain I am sorry forgive me for my abrupt haste." The messenger left as he raced back to Glasgow. He met up with the other messenger who was thrilled with his news to share with the king. The other messenger feared the king's reprisal when he would learn about Uther's disappearance. They both rushed back to Glasgow to deliver their news to the King as the first messenger news was met with excitement the other messenger news was met with utter disbelief Gawain questioned, "What do you mean boy when you say Uther has disappeared?"

 I was told Uther may have been bewitched by the goddess." Gawain still puzzled, "King Uther is missing?"

Gawain could not believe what he was hearing my dear friend is missing. **How can this be? What has happened to him? I know firsthand that Uther is a furious warrior he is not easily beaten** in battle. Gawain pondered further, it must be trickery that is all it could be but who would have that kind of power Merlin, The Lady of Lake, I don't see it they fought side by side against Mab it could not be them. Who else could it be? Come on Gawain think I cannot find the answer I must consult with Tarnish perhaps he could shed some light on this. Gawain left the great hall and headed to Tarnish's quarters. Gawain found Tarnish was nowhere to be found he beckon the page boy where is King Tarnish the page was meager little fellow who was startled when King Gawain spoke to him asking him about Tarnish in a faint whisper he replied, "sir King Tarnish was headed to the courtyard last I saw him."

Gawain headed out to the courtyard Tarnish was walking among the gardens. "Tarnish are you there? Tarnish, come quickly I have grave news Tarnish shocked by Gawain rushed to his side, "Pray dear friend what troubles you so?" Gawain answered back, "It is terrible Tarnish Uther is missing I believe trickery is a foot but I cannot discern the culprit Tarnish what do you think? Who could have done this?"

Tarnish knew more about all of them than Gawain Tarnish contemplated for a moment **who would want to use Uther and why? There are three people that come to mind that have the ability to control others. That is Merlin, Solana, and Helena. I do not believe Solana or Merlin would for one minute use anyone but as for Helena I do not know where her loyalties lie.**

What is reason though? What would prompt her to endanger herself and the tree creatures like that?

"Gawain I believe that Helena is the culprit you seek. Gawain looked to his friend distressed, "We must lay down our grievances with Garlois for now and band together to rescue Uther from the clutches of that vile shrew Helena at once."

"Gawain you are right it is time to take action let us hurry and gather our horde as we intercept Garlois with his company to seek out Uther" Gawain called for the page to fetch the stableman and the castle guard  He told the stableman to saddle the horses. The guard assemble in the main hall Gawain told the men of their peril he looked the men over as he did so Tarnish headed to his quarters and gathered his things.

Gawain knew he would have to leave a throng of men to guard his keep while he was away. Gawain called the four knights that were to battle in the games forward.

"You men will accompany myself and King Tarnish as we head west to intercept King Garlois. As for the rest of you I call upon your pledge of duty to me and the kingdom.  You must defend the court in my absence and carry our banner forward until my return. Do you understand men? The men in unison agreed.

Gawain summoned his page to retrieve the prince from his quarters. The page headed up the spiral staircase to the prince's bed chamber. The page knocked on the massive oak archway doors as he shouted, "King Gawain request your presents in the great hall at once Prince Januarius."...

Januarius was perplexed **why would Gawain request me, he hardly ever acknowledges me at court now he request audience what could this mean?** Januarius was a tall and slender fellow with ginger red hair and bearded face he had a meager build. He arose from bed dressing quickly as he hurried down the stairs to the main hall still pondering **why does he want to see him?** Januarius entered the main hall where he saw the castle guard assembled. The prince bowed in front of King Gawain as he spoke, "You requested to see me your highness"

"Yes brother we must speak in hush tones it has come to my attention that Uther King of the lands to the West has been missing for two moons now. I have arranged to go in search of him with King Tarnish. I have selected a group of knights. I have requested you because I would like to pass the torch to you. I want to name you my brother Januarius as my successor. You are my blood. I trust you with my life will you accept, will you rule in my stead?"

Januarius was stunned by Gawain's news. He would finally have the chance to live the life he was destine for. "Gawain I would be honored to rule in your stead. Dear brother how long to you plan on begin gone? Gawain replied," I do not know but I will not rest until I find Uther. I swore my allegiance to him. Janurius understood Gawain and his oath to Uther as he replied, "Dear brother go in search of your companion I will handle things here, thank you brother."

Janurius come forward he was a frail young man but he was the only blood relative Gawain could trust. Gawain released his sword from its sheath Gawain dubbed Janurius King. All the men bowed Gawain and the other men made their way to the armory to ready themselves for the trip. They headed to the stable where Tarnish was waiting. The men saddled their horses and rode toward the West hoping to meet up with Garlois.

## CHAPTER EIGHT
## THE SEARCH FOR UTHER

Gawain, Tarnish, and the others rode fast and hard trying to reach Garlois's Kingdom before he left. Garlois was preparing his knights for King Gawain's games. Tarnish felt anxious throughout the ride wondering if Garlois would receive them. Tarnish broke formation as he headed toward Gawain. "What are you doing man?" Tarnish replied, "I hope that Garlois will accept us without invitation." Gawain answered back, "Tarnish do not fret we were brothers in arms against Mab and Gallain certainly he would not forget us."

Tarnish and the others bedded for the night and arose before day break. Garlois trained his knights into the wee hours of the eve. He retired to his chamber for some highly needed rest. As he was just about to drift off to slumber. Garlois was awaken by a crashing knock on his chamber door. The castle guard was wrapping on the door. Garlois overtired, "What is it, can I not have a moments peace, Well come in." The guard entered the bed chamber of the king. "Sir Apologies King Gawain and King Tarnish are at the front gate and request audience with you." **What is this about? I answered his request. Why is Tarnish with him?** Garlois pondered for a moment. "Let them in send them to the great hall I will be down as soon as I dress." Tarnish and Gawain were escorted to the great hall by the castle guard. Garlois threw the bed clothes onto the floor. He dressed and made his way to the great hall where Gawain and Tarnish were waiting.

Garlois was known to be a foul tempered person in the morn he was prone to snap at the simplest thing out of place. Gawain spoke first, "Please forgive us for our timing my friend but we have not a moment to lose Uther has gone missing. Tarnish and I have concluded that the vile bitch Helena has taken Uther and is using him for her own devices."

Garlois was puzzled, "What are you saying Uther is missing? Where is Merlin? How could this happened? What would you have me do about it?" Gawain who was appalled at Garlois response began to boil with rage as he heard Garlios utter what would you have me do. Gawain shouted, WHAT CAN YOU DO? Am I hearing you right Garlois? You can aid us in the search for Uther. Garlois how easily you forget if it was not for Tarnish you will still be a cursed man. It was because of him you are here today. Now he calls upon you and your pledge." Garlois stood up as he answered back, "Never it be said that I am not a man of my word Gawain I will aid in your quest but then my pledge is fulfilled. I must ready my Kingdom in my absence do excuse me.

Garlois briskly left Gawain and Tarnish in the great hall. Both Tarnish and Gawain were mystified by the man Garlois had turned out to be it was only a year since they faced Mab and Gallian as allies against evil with Merlin. "Tarnish what he meant when he said his pledge would be fulfilled wonder."

Tarnish looked at Gawain as he replied,
 "Yes I was wondering that myself what are his plans Garlois sure seemed like we were beneath him now and we are all the same. How vain he has become we have no time to dwell on such things we must put our feelings aside for now and find Uther."

Garlois headed to the throne's room where he summoned his knight, Garlois told the men of the recent developments. He told them that Queen Ingrien would rule in his stead. As she was with child her Uncle would act as a liaison but under no circumstances would he have sovereign authority only take orders for Queen Ingrein is that clear. "Yes sir" the knights answered in unison. Garlois chose four of the highest ranked knights to aid in the quest to find Uther they made their way back to the great hall where they were met by Gawain and Tarnish. Garlois never thought he would again wear his battlement armor. A rush of sadness overtook him as he saddled his horse once more. Garlois did not want to leave Ingrein right now. He wanted to be with his love and not search for Uther. Garlois looked back one last time at his castle as he felt a pain in his chest the longing for his wife and their unborn child. A tear fell down his cheek as he rode with his fellow knight in search of Uther. "Well Gawain where are we headed?" Tarnish and Gawain both looked at Garlois as they replied, "We are going back to where it all began. We are going to Avalon in search of Merlin. It is like you said it is very odd that he is not aware of Uther's disappearance."

Merlin astride Pegasus back was still pondering **what happened in his absence? Why would the gods lay waste to the tree creatures? Why would they imprison the animals of war their own creation?** So many questions riddled his mind but all of them were nothing compared to the worry racing through him for Solana.

Helena raced to Uther side she knew she could not hold him forever now that Merlin was back. Helena knew she had to act fast **what can I do I must have Uther in order to free the remaining animals of war.** Helena called to the Phoenix. The Phoenix came down reluctantly, "We must move quickly if we are to free the Manicore do you know where we are to go? The Phoenix told Helena they had to venture deep within the great mountains of Dartmoor

Dartmoor was off to the south purple, heather clad moorland, wide open landscapes, rushing rivers and obscure stone tors shape the landscape of Dartmoor.

There are rolling valleys, bogs and wetland, waterfalls and well-trodden paths. It will be an ominous challenging journey by foot. The Manicore is guarded by trolls." Helena replied, "We must make haste to free the Manicore Phoenix do you have a way to transport us?"

The Phoenix transformed into the fiery bird as she grabbed Helena and Uther she thrust into the air soaring rapidly Uther and Helena dangling in her talon flying over the lush landscapes was but a blur of colors yellow, red and orange surrounded.

Pegasus with Merlin came to the sight of Solana abduction there were no signs of a struggle. Pegasus walked over to the space where Lucifer took Solana he struck his hooves on the ground. The land open beneath his feet as a cavern emerged.

Merlin looked down into the dark ominous expanse searching for any sign of his beloved Solana to no avail it was just a dark treacherous hole Pegasus bent down his head his horn lit up the cavern where Merlin saw a flicker of light a piece of Solana gown was hung on one of the jagged rocks that protruded in the expanse, "Pegasus we must hurry let us go!"

Pegasus and Merlin jumped into the cavern it seems if they were free falling forever until they saw the bottom it was false charcoaled shale. As soon as Pegasus foot touch it the ground caved in and molten silver shot upwards barely missing Merlin and Pegasus. Merlin called on the elements of water his eyes changed to an electric blue he waved his hands as surges of water jettison from his palms. The water made a thunderous splash it harden the silver liquid.

Merlin dismounted Pegasus as he raced through the cavern running at full speed. Pegasus on the other hand treaded slowly begin cautious. He knew that Lucifer was cunning as well as devious. Pegasus wanted to be on his guard to make sure Merlin nor himself would fall into a trap.

Merlin becoming more anxious by the minute he cried out, "Pegasus we have not time to waste we must find Solana I feel her she is close by but she is weak Hurry Pegasus." Solana was unconscious as Merlin and Pegasus approached the oval glass prison of Solana.

Merlin looked at her breathtaking beauty as her long flowing hair floated in the air. Her body lay motionless. Merlin looked closer at his beloved whose face was covered in a veil. **Why her beautiful face is covered** he thought. Pegasus cautioned Merlin to be careful for all is not what it seems. Merlin too sensed something was amiss. Merlin pick up a rock and threw it at Solana prison.

As the rock sailed towards the oval glass prison it was deflected branches of thorns and thistles arose from the ground encompassing Solana's prison. Beams of light bright red shot through the air as they encircled Solana's prison placing a strong force field barrier around it as well. Pegasus looked to Merlin, "I can break through the barrier as well as the thistle and thorns.

Pegasus told Merlin he could eat them Merlin it is up to you to break the glass oval and the steel bounds that enslave Solana." Merlin did not hesitate as beckoned Pegasus to hurry. Pegasus lowered his head his horn began to glow a fire red as he charged into the force field shattering the barrier. Pegasus plunged his powerful jaws into the thorns and thistles devouring them in seconds.

Merlin burst into action as he sent a lightning bolt directly into the center of the glass oval. The lightning bolt hit the chains and lock melting it completely but the glass remained unchanged. Merlin again tried to break the oval glass prison to no avail.

Pegasus looked to Merlin, "You will not be able to penetrate her prison Merlin. It is just as I feared Lucifer has imprisoned her in a prison that was forged by the gods. It can only be broken by the chosen one with the sword of the ancient and the jewel of time"

Merlin was infuriated as he shouted, "Damn the gods and their power I am Merlin the Magi Dragon and they will set Solana free now!" Merlin tapped into all his power as he focused all his energy his body became to shake his veins bulged his eyes became enlarged as he called on all the elements his magi powers as he centered all that power toward Solana's oval glass prison the massive converge of power erupted from Merlin as a giant shockwaves were sent to Solana prison it began to crack and break apart. Solana was free at last.

Merlin raced to her side. He reach to embrace her. She was so frail Merlin wanted to make sure her delicate body would not hit the cold hard ground. As he held her to him Merlin began to unravel the veil to discover her terrible secret. Solana's once beautiful face was scar covered in boils and pock marks. Merlin was enraged to see his beloved in this state. She was still unconscious Solana was cold and her skin was colorless. Solana was near death. Merlin tried to revive her but Solana did not respond. Merlin was on the brink of madness he took out the ruby dagger. *I must do it I must save her* was all that weighed on his mind.

Merlin cut at his flesh. The green emerald blood trickled out and drip onto Solana lifeless lips. The blood crept into her mouth Solana eyes began to flutter her body stirred as her eyes flew wide open and rolled into the back of her head as she tasted the blood Solana arose in Merlin arms Solana sank her teeth into his wound. She drank of him her body jerked and contorted Merlin struggled trying to break free from Solana. Pegasus watch as Merlin was struggling with Solana.

He charged in between the two of them breaking their embrace. Solana fell to the ground like a sack of potatoes with a loud thud. As soon as she impacted with the ground her sense started to come back to her. Solana looked up to see her beloved Merlin. Solana felt the wind on her face and knew her dreadful secret had been discovered as she try to cover up her shame with her hands. When Solana began to feel her face it was smooth. She grasped her cheek where the horrible scar was to find it was no longer there. Solana reached from a piece of that vile oval prison holding it closed to her she gently moved it closer to her face as she looked into it her eyes widen with joy for her beautiful face was again returned to her. Solana looked to Merlin rubbing her eyes to make sure it was not another dream.

She was overjoyed to see him once again. Solana filled with warmth at the site of her darling Merlin. Is it really you Merlin I cannot believe my eyes. Merlin have you finally returned to me at last!"

Merlin's mind was set at ease when he heard his sweet Lady of Lake speak to him once as he replied, "Yes dear heart it is I" Merlin reached both his arms out to embrace her that is when Solana realized her disgrace as Merlin's forearm was covered in his emerald green blood. Solana was filled with remorse for what she had done her eyes started to burn as tears started to fall down her face she ran to Merlin's arms.

"Please dear heart forgive me. I am sorry I drank of your life-force" Merlin held her tight to his chest as he caressed her face. "Hush my love it is alright" as he bent down and cupped Solana's face in his hands as he tenderly kiss her luscious lips. Merlin was at last happy but only for a moment because just as the two of them were reunited Lucifer appeared with his minions.

Freyja the Valkyrie herself astride her black wolf. Botis at Freyja's left a giant man with two sharp horns protruding from his head his carnivorous mouth with huge canines. Eligos is a warrior knight astride his winged horse.

Pegasus flew into action as Lucifer and his minions lead an all-out assault on Merlin and Solana. Pegasus raised his wings as he flapped them he released his feather.
Plums of feathers as sharp as daggers aimed at the attackers. Solana called upon her power as the crescent moon began to draw strength her eyes grew enlarged as she sent a towering waves of water into the small crevasse the impact of the waves sent Lucifer and his minions to the four winds.

Merlin levitated out of the way of the tidal waves as did Solana. Solana and Merlin were depleted as Pegasus flew down to save them. They landed on his back as he thrust into the air. The cavern started to crumple all round them.

Pegasus was flying hard and fast dodging falling rocks he caused a vortex closing the opening forever. They soared out of the cavern at last. The Phoenix, Uther, and Helena arrived at the peaks of Dartmoor. The landscape ahead was treacherous indeed with the steep cliff, deep chasm, jagged rocks, and slippery slopes.

Helena was freezing at the snow covered mountain peak. The Phoenix looked to Helena as she shouted, "We have no time to waste Helena call upon your powers over the earth and hurry." Helena was shivering with cold as she tried to focus her energy deep down within the mountain.

Helena thrust her hand down opening the mountain as the earth shook piles of rock and soil came streaming out of the ground like a hot geyser. Helena deflected the debris over the mountain side.

Uther stood motionless under Helena's trance. The Phoenix hovered over wait to see her friend released. Helena finished clearing out the path to the Manicore's prison but that was only half of the battle for the inside of the mountain was a stronghold of trolls that guarded the Manicore.

Dovregubben was the king of all the trolls. Most trolls were shaggy and rough-haired, with trees and moss-like growth on their heads and noses. Their noses were long and they would stir with it when cooking broth or porridge. Some even had two or three heads, some only had one eye in the middle of their foreheads. Their features differed from humans with four fingers and four toes and a tail resembling that of a cow.

Helena grabbed Uther and headed down onto the pathway. It was pitch black, Helena was unable to see anything in front of her she beckons the Phoenix to come down to light the way. The Phoenix transformed into human form she covered herself with flames as she entered the passage. The three of them walked with caution not to arouse the attention of the trolls.

The pathway itself was very arduous the ground below their feet was slimy gooey mud that sloshed at every step the further they

went the more perils they ran into to if the mud was not bad enough the jagged rocks were a nightmare. Cutting and tearing at their flesh with scrapes and cuts they pressed on until they reached an alcove.
 This was the troll's stronghold large hairy foul smelling men that reeked of blood and scum. Helena approached carefully scouting the area. The trolls lived in a honeycomb structured maze scattered throughout Helena watched the guards would patrol the Manicore's prison.

The Manicore's prison was like nothing she has seen before. A large pyramid shape was elevated in the air above a large pit filled with snakes. The pyramid was made of limestone. It had a protective force field around it. As one of the guards stumbled and was instantly shot into the air about forty feet.

The Manicore's prison seemed unbreakable. The trolls surrounded it at the ready for attack. They guarded it in shifts each guard carried a large battle axe. As one shift retired there was another taking over three guard to every side of the pyramid as Helena scouted further not only were the trolls guarding the ground level but they also guarded above too.
Helena knew the only way they would succeed was a sneak attack at the changing of the guard. They would have to bide their time and wait to make their presents known.

Garlois, Gawain, and Tarnish headed towards Avalon they rode long into the night before they reached the shoreline of the majestic lake. All the men were fatigued they decided to make camp for the night. Each man took a task to set up camp.

Gawain went in search of game in the woods. Garlois looked for a place to secure the horses. Tarnish gathered twigs, sticks, logs and flint to build a fire. The majestic lake between worlds was full of mist. Gawain hunted like a true woodsmen back in his element of the forest. He felt right at home as he searched the ground for the foot prints of wild game.

Garlois found the perfect place to tie the horses and bed for the night. A flat piece of Earth covered with thick grass so their slumber would not be a discomfort. Tarnish headed back to the majestic lake looking for Garlois. He waved his hand to show he was friend as he approached the camp site.

Tarnish carried a bundle of twigs in his hand with stacks of logs on both sides of his arms Tarnish collected pieces of flint as well and tucked them into his gunny sack.

Tarnish placed all the fire logs down as he started to build the fire Tarnish spoke, "All is ready to build the fire where is Gawain with that game?" Garlois was too growing concerned about Gawain as he replied, "you are right Tarnish he should have been back by now. Besides I am ravenous I could eat anything right now." Tarnish chuckled, "As could I Garlois what could be keeping him?

Gawain hunted like a true predator he would spy on his prey waiting to strike at the best moment and he would lung into an attack before the animal had time to react. Gawain was upon them with one thrust of his blade he would take the animals life leaving no trace. Gawain captured three dear and two rabbits. *I should head back to camp and save some sport for the morn.*

Gawain took hold of his kills and carried back to camp. The men cleaned and gutted the prey as they placed them over the fire the smell of their burning flash delighted the hungry men they ate their fill and drifted off to sleep.

They arose with the morn sun rise and could not believe what their sight beheld. The once clear flowing lake had turned black. The beautiful lush green valley was devoid of vegetation. The towing picturesque oak trees were dying as if the land and Avalon were connected somehow.

Galois spoke up, "Well we are here Gawain not what?" Gawain was puzzled on what to do next. Tarnish spoke up, "Garlois you must be patient for Gawain has all in hand he will summon Merlin." Gawain had no idea how to summon Merlin. The last time he was in Avalon Uther had brought him. Gawain tried to think of what Uther did to summon Merlin, Gawain ponder for a few moments as he concentrated on Merlin.

Gawain called out "MERLIN MERLIN WE HAVE COME TO AVALON IN NEED OF YOUR HELP!!! MERLIN CAN YOU HEAR ME!!" Tarnish and Garlois looked upon their friend shouting to the wind call out to Merlin both were dubious of Gawain's tack. Then in a faint whisper was heard by all three men "Yes Gawain I hear you. Why are you at Avalon?"
All three men were in disbelief their eyes grew enlarged as Gawain answered, "Uther has been kidnapped. We have band together Merlin in search of our missing companion. We fear that Helena is behind it casting a spell on Uther controlling him." Merlin was outraged, "WHAT I just saw Helena Gawain I will get to the bottom of this wait for me at Avalon. Solana and Pegasus are on their way to you." Gawain replied back, "Yes Merlin we will await you here." Merlin rushed to his beloved side "Solana we must hurry we have no time you must flee back to Avalon. Gawain and the others are waiting for you there. Uther has gone missing they believe Helena is the cause.

 Solana bowed her head in shame as she started to cry, "Yes Merlin it is true Helena has Uther under an enchantment she needs him to release the animals of war. She wants to overthrow Mt. Olympus for their cruelty and destruction of the tree creatures. Merlin I am so sorry I let my emotions for you cloud my judgement. I just wanted you at whatever cost. I formed an alliance with Helena to gain access to the jewels of time so that I

could travel through time to find you Merlin. Please forgive me dear heart."
Merlin could not believe what he was hearing. His beloved was willing to sacrifice another to find him. She pledged herself to Helena's quest in order to find him.

Merlin was conflicted because he was no better he put himself in danger seeking vengeance for his family only to learn it was pointless. He left Solana in a fit of rage fuelled by hate so in turn he must forgive her. "Solana dearest I too have wronged in this and must atone for my faults but right now we must find Helena. Where is she now? Pegasus spoke up, "She was on the ridge last I seen her Merlin"
 Merlin replied, "Solana you must go back to Avalon with Pegasus and hurry."

Solana climbed atop Pegasus back. Pegasus began to gallop as his stride grew faster Pegasus leapt into the air his massive wings flapping rapidly as they soared into the clouds. Solana was holding onto Pegasus mane for dear life as the landscape below was but a blur. It seemed as if hours went by in the blink of an eye.
They arrived in Avalon in a matter of moments. Gawain and the other knights were astride their horses waiting on the outskirts of Avalon. Pegasus dove down from the heavens. The men froze in fear of Pegasus this magnificent flying horned horse.

The men dismounted ready for attack as Pegasus set to land Garlois grabbed the hilt of his sword ready to attack. Tarnish was in awe of this striking sight of horseflesh. Gawain bowed to the ground to show his homage to the Pegasus. Solana dismounted quickly as Pegasus bellowed, "Please men do not attack. I come only to aid you not to fight."

The men stood bewildered as the horse spoke unaware on how to react they awaited word from Solana. Solana was overjoyed to see the knights as she address them, "Garlois, Gawain, and Tarnish it seems ages since I have last looked upon your faces. Merlin has sent me here to ease your minds knights as you know Uther has been kidnapped by Helena it is true. Gawain answered back, "What are we to do where Uther is so that we may aid in his rescue dear lady. Solana countered, "Merlin has that in hand sir Gawain please await his instruction on this matter. I am here to offer accommodation so you may seek refuge in Avalon until Merlin reveals his new directive to follow."

Solana placed her hands on the misty veil between worlds as she raised her hands upward and in a circular motion she parted the veil between worlds to Avalon. Solana ran to her home as she enter the sanctuary the withered and dying plants started to heal and bloom. The landscape changed the dark roaring waters of the majestic lake ran clear. The gloomy crumbling fortress started to morph into the pristine ivory castle it once was. Tarnish Garlois Gawain and Pegasus followed Solana to Avalon.

Merlin went in search of Helena, Uther, and the Phoenix on the ridge. He search for any sign and found none at all. Merlin tried to use his powers over the mind to link to Uther's minds eyes but whatever enchantment Helena used it by passed his link to Uther.

Merlin was so defeated he began to ponder **What can I do? I must find Uther before Helena is able to go fourth with her plans to overthrow Mt. Olympus. I have to find a way to forgive Solana for her faults in this they were not her doing alone. I love her more that life itself and I was foolish to break our bond chasing after Desmoria. Oh my damn morality who am I to cast judgement upon her for trying to reunite us. Damn Desmoria for this and Helena I hope they both enjoy Hades for that is where they are to be tormented for eternity for the terror they yielded here on Earth.**

## *CHAPTER NINE*
## *THE MANICORE RELEASE*

Helena headed back to the others in the tunnel Uther stood motionless under Helena's spell. The Phoenix was growing restless waiting for Helena to return. She paced back and forth it seemed like hours which in fact was only about five minutes.

Helena moved swiftly through the tunnel when she approached the Phoenix she whispered, "I have seen the troll's lair there are a great many of them in number. I have seen the Manicore prison and I assure you it is going to be hard to break the Manicore free." The Phoenix was not deterred on her course to set he dear friend of the Manicore free. "I am sure that for you it may seem difficult Helena but I am not the least bit worried about freeing the Manicore. Those trolls stand no threat to my power I assure you. When can we make our attempt?"

Helena was growing more and more anger with every word that the Phoenix uttered. "I believe our best chance is at the changing of the guard. We must strike then. The prison itself is triangular and is bolted on all three sides with a thick heavy chain. It floats atop a pit of snakes. Oh yes and there is a force field around it. Not to mention it is guarded by trolls on all side and above. But for you Phoenix it is piece of cake."

The Phoenix too was tired of this repartee and wanted to take action as soon as possible. The Phoenix was proud warrior and that got the better of her at times when she heard Helena explain everything she started to doubt her ability to free her friend alone as she answered back, "What do you suggest Helena for I was swept away at the thought of the Manicore being free like myself."

Helena looked to the Phoenix as she counter, "Tonight at dusk we will make our assault I will lead Uther through the tunnel to the prison of the Manicore in disguise so that we do not attract attention. You Phoenix must find a way to penetrate the force field so that Uther can break the chains. Meanwhile I will call upon the tree roots to break through the prison. Once the prison is broken the Manicore will be lifted by the tree roots to the surface. You Phoenix will transform into the fiery bird you will grab Uther and myself as we jettison to the surface where you can reunite with the Manicore."

The Phoenix agreed to wait until dusk for to launch the attack. Helena led Uther down the tunnel until they were right outside the troll's lair. Helena chanted the spell of glamorous, "When the moon strikes down
Make the change from below Trolls
become visible to all as we take the form of Trolls disguise us now this I call." Uther and she were transformed into trolls. She picked up mud and smeared it on herself and Uther to cover up their smell. Both of them headed to the changing of the guard. Helena told Uther to head toward the chains and wait. Uther moved toward the chain and waited. The Phoenix followed as she spied the prison where her dear friend had been held all these years.

The Phoenix focused all her power to the center of the prison hoping it would break the force field that surrounded it. She waited for Helena to give her indication on when to strike. Helena watched as the trolls started to walk off their post she shot her hand into the air in one motion. The Phoenix sent a towering stream of flames towards the center of the Manicore prison all the trolls saw the light from the fire and were turned to stone. Helena motioned to Uther.

Uther grabbed Excalibur from his scabbard as he thrust the might sword of power into the air he charged the steel blade down onto the chains. Once the sword impacted the chains it burst into flames.

Helena drew upon her powers calling to the tree roots nestled into the ground. "I call upon you great Oak brother the mighty Sycamore sister raise up this day. I, Helena call upon you raise up evermore from the harden ground reach to the sky. From down deep I reach my hands to your roots come fourth brother and sister this I cry."

Helena who stood near the edge of the tunnel pulled out her dagger and pricked her finger to cause a bead of blood to pool. She plunged her hand deep within the Earth as she touched the Oak and Sycamore roots with the bead of blood. The roots started to grow at a quickened pace. Surging up from the ground forward the roots raced toward the top of the snake pit.

Uther cut down the massive prison where the Manicore was housed. An explosion was heard deep within the Earth as the great oak and mighty sycamore arose from the snake pit. The tree roots were just in time to catch the massive prison before it lowered to the ground. Helena raced to Uther and grabbed him in the nick of time before the towering roots emerged. The Phoenix transformed into the fiery bird and whisked them upwards with the tree roots as the trolls lair was turned to rumble in an instant.

Merlin stood on the ridge looking for any sign of Helena or Uther when he felt the Earth tremble as a giant shockwave was felt across the land. This must be the work of Helena. Merlin focused his powers on the shockwave. He concentrated all his powers on the Earth. As flame lights shadow,
and truth ends fear. Open lost thoughts to my minds willing ear. Show me the force that caused the Earth to tremble and shake so that I, Merlin may combat this unnatural wake. Merlin mind's eye open to the dark recess of Dartmoor deep within the mountain side he saw a glimpse of Vibrate Orange and ruby red flames as they soared to the surface. Massive tree roots of the great oak and mighty sycamore arose unnatural colossal in size to the top of the mountain where Merlin caught sight of Helena an Uther and strange triangular pyramid entangled in the great oak and mighty sycamore tree roots. Just as Merlin was about to leave his mind's eye he beheld the sight of the fiery bird again. Merlin consider his options carefully after he learned the whereabouts of Uther.

  **I must move quickly to put an end to Helena's plans. She had managed to free the Phoenix, Pegasus and now she is on top of Mt. Dartmoor with what I believe to be the prison of one more of the animals of war. Think Merlin what is the best course in this before I go off into danger unknown I must return to Avalon I must gather forces to end this madness once and for all Helena must be stopped.** Merlin transformed into a dragon and flew towards Avalon.

Solana await Merlin she knew she would have to consult the goddess soon. Solana needed to find a way to combat Helena's enchantment over Uther. Garlois, Gawain, and Tarnish were grow more and more impatient awaiting Merlin. Gawain was the first to speak his mind, "Tarnish and Garlois I say we take action we are not silly women we need no accommodation. We need to find Uther where the devil is Merlin anyway he should have been here by now." Garlois countered, "Even if we head out in search of Uther we have no idea where to look." Tarnish came back with, "I know it is trying to wait I too am growing edgy but Garlois is right we have no idea where Uther is. It is best we wait for Merlin."

Gawain shouted, "Damn this I cannot just sit here. I must do something the more we wait the harder it will be to find Uther." The three men sat in the sanctuary of Avalon. Pegasus knew it was only a matter of time before his plans would be foiled by Merlin. He needed a way to persuade Merlin to his favor and join his quest.

Pegasus was not one to fear a god or goddess but Merlin was so much more than that. Pegasus told the others he was going to scout the perimeter and then return. He needed to get out of the sanctuary he felt like a trapped beast once again.
Solana told him to go. "Pegasus please return by night fall for the veil will close by then." Pegasus agreed as he flew up into the heavens once again. Solana rushed into the secret chamber of the goddess to call upon her. Solana bowed at the altar and placed several gifts upon it for the goddess. She placed two candles at each end of the alter. Solana began to chant I am good, "I am clean, I call to you goddess you are my fifth element unseen

accept these gifts that you see in return, please goddess come to me. I am your vessel I am your tool please come to me goddess."

The winds started to sweep through the chamber as the candles went dark flashes of light filled the chamber as a puff of smoke appeared a blaze of fire sparked as the goddess appeared. The goddess was weary she had not healed from her last encounter with Merlin as the marks on her neck were still fresh. "Solana you beckon me what has happened? I thought you had forsaken your oath for love. I believe you denounced Avalon. What do you need of me?"
Solana still kneeling bowed her head as she spoke goddess, "I was a fool I let my emotions rule my head. It is true I denounced Avalon and you but I was fool hearty in my decision. I have cause a world of chaos since I left. Goddess I pledged myself to Helena and her quest to usurp Mt Olympus I aided in freeing the Phoenix with Pegasus Helena and Uther. I am not worthy of you grace goddess. I am bewildered for Helena has cast a spell upon Uther controlling his every move. He is her puppet to do with as she wants. I beg of you goddess please help me lift the enchantment upon him so that Helena's plan will be foiled and we can return to peace and harmony back to the land once again."

The Goddess was livid at the confession of Solana. The goddess choose her above all others to be her vessel. It be so callous to be so easily lead for love. What could she be thinking? The goddess would never understand this feeling of love.

"Solana you dare to aid Helena in her quest to destroy Mt Olympus. You freed the Phoenix with Pegasus this is an outrage you defy the gods for your selfish ends Solana how could you?" Solana knew the goddess was angry and she did not want to enrage her any more she begged for forgiveness she pleaded for the goddess to show her favor.

The goddess knew that she must intervene before it was too late. She knew that two of the animals of war were release. She did not have the privilege to inflict her retribution now so she would move to end this farce of a quest before Mt Olympus was ruined forever.

"You say that Helena had a spell on Uther she has control over his every action. You said he is like her puppet bending to her will. I must consult the oracle to find the answer for which you seek. Pray tell me Merlin is here for only he will be able to wield such a charm."

Solana replied yes goddess he is back but he went in search of Helena I do not know when he will return to Avalon." the goddess replied," Summon him Solana tell him about what I have told you and wait for me to return within the next phased of the moon."  Solana answered back, "Yes, goddess I will thank you goddess for your grace thank you for a second chance to be your vessel I will never again fail you."

As soon as Solana finished talking the goddess disappeared from sight. Solana knew she must reach Merlin. Solana started to focus her mind on her beloved. Solana drew deeper into her mind she collected her thoughts on Merlin. Solana's mind's eye opened as she spoke softly calling out to Merlin. In the hint of a whisper "Merlin my love can you hear Merlin please return to Avalon Merlin can you hear me." Merlin was on his way back to Avalon to figure out a way to break the enchantment spell that Helena had on Uther when he heard Solana voice. "Solana I hear you I am coming to Avalon right now I am on my way I should be there by night fall."

Pegasus was flying overhead circling at first to avoid suspicion then he moved further and further from Avalon. Pegasus raced to Dartmoor where he knew the Phoenix, Helena, and Uther would venture next to release the Manicore.

Pegasus knew that he must persuade Merlin that he was only a pawn in Helena's quest. When actually he was the mastermind. He must lure him back to Dartmoor and away from Avalon. Pegasus saw Merlin in the distance flying toward Avalon shores.

Pegasus had to think fast he raced into Merlin's flight path "Merlin we must head to Dartmoor to rescue Uther I have a plan Merlin come with me so we can end this." Merlin did not veer off his course Pegasus pleaded with Merlin to join him. Merlin refused, "It will only lead to trouble if we go to Dartmoor alone Pegasus we must return to Avalon with Solana and the others. We can plan our attack. You understand let us head back now Pegasus."

Pegasus knew Merlin would not be dissuaded from his course you leave me no choice Merlin Pegasus reared up and charged at Merlin. Merlin was not the best flyer and not as skilled at Pegasus. Merlin dove down to avoid Pegasus attack. Merlin counter as he began to breathe fire into his lungs. He spun around releasing fire from his mouth directed at Pegasus.

 Pegasus dodged the fire stream from Merlin. He flapped his wings rapidly into the air causing strong Gail force winds trying to send Merlin to the ground. Merlin again shot massive fireballs in Pegasus direction. The massive winds from Pegasus put out the fireballs before they could reach him.

Pegasus was through playing around. He went in for the kill if he could not have Merlin at his side he would not allow him to live. Pegasus released his feathers into the air like steel daggers headed straight for Merlin as they whistled in the air. Merlin saw them out of the corner of his eye.  Merlin began to fly upward toward the steel feathers gaining speed. Merlin led his final attack on Pegasus. Merlin knew his best bet was to let Pegasus believe he had the upper hand so he would let his guard down.

Pegasus release his feathers which made him vulnerable to attack. Merlin flew hard and fast now heading straight for Pegasus. Merlin went into a barrel roll avoiding the steel feather daggers. Pegasus used his energy and focused all his power onto his golden horn calling upon the powers of Zeus's mighty thunderbolt.

With all his might Pegasus sent a colossal lightning bolt toward Merlin. Merlin dodge the lightning bolt as he sank his talons into Pegasus. Pegasus tried to break free of the Merlin's grip.

They fought against one another in a powerful embrace. Merlin tearing at the flesh of Pegasus. Pegasus took all the strength he could muster forcing his wings to open knocking Merlin's grip free. Pegasus knew he would not win this battle so with all he had left in him Pegasus retreated to higher ground flying towards Mt Dartmoor.

Merlin was thrown from Pegasus about fifty feet. He was free falling hindered unconscious from the battle. As he fell thru the air the wind surging all around him. Merlin heard a faint voice Merlin, Merlin....... Merlin where are you? The sound of the faint voice stunned Merlin awake just as he was about to collide with the mountain side. Merlin took control flying fast and hard in the direction of Avalon. "Merlin where are you?" The voice beckoned.

Merlin answered, "I am headed to Avalon I am headed to you." The voice was hard to discern as it replied, "I am not in Avalon Merlin." Merlin was stunned who this could be talking to him. Merlin perplexed asked, "Who is this reveal yourself to me?"

"Merlin it is I, Uther Penedragon I am at Dartmoor I need you help!!!!! I have been enchanted by Helena I am unable to control myself but I am trying to break her charm upon me. Help me Merlin she has grave plans for this world and the gods Hurry Merlin......" the voice trailed off.

Uther we are coming, we will save you! "Merlin headed to Avalon with haste. Solana told the others about her meeting with the goddess. She explained that Merlin was on his way and would be in Avalon around nightfall.

Gawain interjected, "Solana the last time we faced Helena she was a force to be reckoned with. Now not only do we have to contend with her but with animals of war as well. I fear our chances Lady of Lake. Solana counter, "Don't you see that is why I enlisted the help of the goddess to aid us in rescuing Uther from Helena's clutches to stop her before she releases the animals of war. Tarnish retorted we only know of one animal of war that has been released and that was Pegasus and he seems no threat to us. Galois responded, "That is true Tarnish he was no threat to us as of yet."

Solana answered back with, "Yes I can confirm that two animals of war have been released. Do not take them lightly they are a threat to us and the gods themselves. I know Helena's plan the goddess will help us to free Uther. She has gone to the oracle to seek the potion to break the enchantment over Uther."

Merlin was the horizon of Avalon he could see the veil between worlds. Merlin flew through the veil and headed straight for the sanctuary. Just as the men were about to confront Solana Merlin burst in on them. The men were all taken back by the sight of Merlin they forgot about their dissatisfaction with Solana. Gawain addressed Merlin, At last you are here Merlin now we can take action. Tell us Merlin what news do you have about Uther?"

Tarnish Interjected, "Yes Merlin tell us what is our next move. We are anxious to rescue our friend before he is put in danger. Merlin pray tell us what to do so that we may free our friend from the vile clutches of Helena." Garlois remained silent awaiting Merlin's news.

"It is true I know where Helena is and her plans to overthrow Mt Olympus. She has captured Uther. I have spoken to him. He pleaded for us to help him break Helena enchantment. I am sorry to say I don't know how to break this powerful enchantment."

Solana interjected, "No need to worry my love for the goddess has pledged her aid she went in seek of the oracle and will return within a cycle of the moon with the potion to break Uther's spell." Gawain was fluster with all this talk he wanted action as he asked "Well Merlin what will you have us do in the mean time?" Merlin knew they had to act fast to gain control of Uther before Helena, Pegasus, and the Phoenix could further their plans.

"What would I have you do indeed? Gawain you and the other knights need to ride to Dartmoor. Gawain you must recapture

Uther and bring him back to Avalon. I know this will not be an easy task for any of you. I have thought of this long and hard as I was flying back here. The animals of war are a true enemy that is for sure. Come closer knights I want to anoint your armor and swords so that you may defeat the Phoenix and Pegasus. Solana I need your help in this join hands with me."

Merlin with his free hand pointed downward. Merlin sent a powerful light through his index finger as he drew a pentagram on the floor. He levitated candles from the sanctuary and placed them on all five points of the pentagram. Gawain Tarnish and Garlois moved to the center of the pentagram. Merlin drew upon the power within. Solana did the same as her half-moon crescent began to glow. Merlin's eyes started to change as his fangs started to protrude from his upper lip. Merlin started to chant "Thrice around the circles bound sink all evil to the ground protect this armor with all you might oh goddess gracious day and night."

Merlin chanted this five times as he utter the final chant all the candles started to go out one by one the pentagram began to glow in a rainbow of color blue, red, and green encompass the men as they stood in the circle.

A flash of purple light exploded as the men's armor were purified with a protective shield. The swords of the men were coated with an amber shine. The shields of the knights were also coated with the amber shine. Solana bellowed, "Go fourth knights and seek out Uther you are protected by the gods hurry now." The knights raced to their horses riding off towards Dartmoor. Gawain was racing to his friend hopeful that they would be able to rescue him from Helena's spell. Garlois rode cautiously because he knew his companions fate lay in his hands. Garlois knew the battle would not be easy he worried that Helena would have the upper hand with the animals of war and herself it was sure to be a blood bath at any rate.

Tarnish was so eager to rescue Uther he did not think about the animals of war or Helena only that he must save Uther at any cost. The Knights rode through the evening early the next morn they were all exhausted and famished with hunger. Garlois was the first to speak up.

"I cannot ride another second I must rest my weary bones." Gawain was also done in as he replied, "Aye it has been a long ride let us dismount here." Tarnish agreed, "Yes it sounds a good plan to me. I will gather some fire wood." Gawain replied, "Aye I will hunt and get us some game to fill our bellies. Garlois began to set up camp as he took the horses to water. Gawain dismounted and headed into the forest scanning the land for animal tracks, droppings, as well as fur. Gawain spotted broken tree branches and cloven hoof prints in the forest floor. There was no doubt about it these were the telltale signs of a Boar.

The Boar was a highly dangerous animal to hunt; it would fight ferociously when under attack, and could easily kill a dog, a horse, or a man. It was hunted *par force*, and when at bay, a hound like a mastiff could perhaps be foolhardy enough to attack it, but ideally it should be killed by a rider with a spear. The boar was considered a malicious animal. Gawain had no such luxury at his disposal.

All he had was his wits and strength to hunt this boar. Gawain walked softly in the wood trying to find the boars den hoping to take the animal by surprise armed with his mighty broad sword and trusty dagger. Gawain began to smell the pungent order of boar droppings a fresh steaming pile of boar excrement lay on the path. *This is fresh the Boar must be close by.* Gawain with his sword at the ready he heard a crackling in the bushes. The Boar came charging out ready to attack. Gawain with sword in hand stuck the boar wounding it. The boar squealed out in pain but was not deterred in his mission to lay waste to Gawain as the turn to charge again.

Gawain saw his opportunity to attack, he ran toward the massive Boar with his dagger in hand. Gawain struck the final blow straight into the heart of the Boar. The Boar felt the immense pain as the blood started to gush out of him. The Boar lay motionless as darkness overtook the animal and the light was gone forever. Gawain was pleased with himself. Gawain let the animal bleed out he hoisted upon his shoulders and carried it back to camp. Tarnish gather wood and started to build a fire. Garlois took the horses to water as he filled his rucksack as well as the others for it was still about a three days ride to Dartmoor. Gawain met Tarnish as he had set the fire a blaze. "Good man getting the fire going now help me unmake this boar so we can feast." Tarnish was astonished to see Gawain single handedly killed this massive Boar "WOW I am going to send you to the wood more often." Aye he is a beauty the fight was electrifying. It is good to fill the spark of life again within me." Tarnish saw the wry smile on Gawain's face laughing, "Yes it does you justice indeed my friend now let hurry with the unmaking of this boar so we can set it a roast upon the fire pit. Garlios ventured into the wood forging for berries, roots, and herbs for the long journey.

Garlois began to smell the succulent aroma of roasted meat. He followed the sent back to camp where Tarnish and Gawain were waiting the chance to feast on the Boar. Garlios gather nuts, berries, parsnips, apples, and herbs. "I see you have been busy while I water and fed the horses. Gawain that is a mighty prize boar you captured it will just suffice us on a journey. All the men feasted and fell fast asleep. Merlin was gathering his strength. He knew that time was of the essences. War was coming so he must make ready for battle. Merlin had never faced such villains as the animals of war. Pegasus, the Phoenix, the Manicore, and Leviathan. Merlin knew Pegasus was a mighty opponent that was skilled in the art of war. The Phoenix as well was a force to be reckoned with.

 Merlin racked his brain trying to find a way to defeat these giant beasts. Merlin needed to know as much as he could about his enemy so he asked Solana to tell him all she knew of the animals of war.

Solana explained that her knowledge was limited. "My father told me tales as a child about the mighty animals of war. They are fables Merlin there is no truth in them as far as I know." Well let me be the judge of that Solana tell me the stories so I can better judge our enemy."

"Well let me think for a moment my father told of the great Pegasus when I was a child. Pegasus was an immortal, winged horned horse which sprang forth from the neck of Medousa when she was beheaded by the hero Perseus. Pegasus was tamed by Bellerophon, a Korinthian hero, who rode him into battle against the fire-breathing Khimaira. Later, after the hero attempted to fly to heaven, the gods caused the horse to buck, throwing him back down to Earth. Pegasus continued to wing its way to heaven where it took a place in the stables of Zeus. As such he was often named thunderbolt-bearer of Zeus." Merlin interjected. "Yes Solana please go on we have to hurry what else can you tell me about the Animals of War."

Helena told me about the Phoenix. She was a beautiful women with scarlet red and blond hair her beauty was known far and wide throughout the land. Her beauty would be a downfall for it was said that the Phoenix was more beautiful than the goddess. This enraged the goddess to be compared to a mortal.

The goddess tried to burn the beautiful mortal known as the Phoenix. Zeus saw what the goddess was trying to do so he intervened. As the Phoenix was set ablaze with the fire of the gods Zeus sent down his massive thunderbolt causing the beautiful maiden to embrace the fire and transform it into this massive

winged bird. The giant firebird soared to the heaven and stood beside Pegasus and the other animals of war.
As a titian for the gods the Phoenix would set ablaze to villages leaving ash and smoke in its wake. If a mortal would to look upon the Phoenix their eyes were burn out rendering them to blind. The Phoenix songs would make mortal's ears bleed.

Merlin interrupted, "This is good to know what of the Manicore and Leviathan?" All I know about The Manicore is that it is a vile beast with the body of lion, the wings of a dragon, and the tail of a scorpion. The Manicore was created by Lucifer to strike fear in the hearts of all men. In the stories of old it was said that Pegasus grew tired of being a play thing for the gods and rebelled with the Phoenix, the Manicore and the Leviathan.

The gods knew that the animals of war separately were no threat but when united they are all powerful and needed to be imprisoned for the safety of the land. Zeus and the other gods fought with the animals of war trapping them in their prisons forever never to be heard of again only in the legends would they remain. Merlin thought to himself **I must find a way to trap them like the gods did so many years ago. But how what could hold them and keep them like the prison? I've got it there is only one thing that will bind them together in harmony I will create a tome of my dragon skin. I will trap the animals of war forever in this tome. They will be free to roam the land I will not imprison them like before.**
Gawain, Tarnish, and Garlois rode trying to catch up with Helena. As they rode they planned their attack Gawain spoke up

first, "The best way to attack Helena was to surprise her she cannot have time to conjure up a plan, she must be taken out first. Tarnish replied, "Yes I agree with that but we must meet up with Merlin and Solana before we go on the attack. Garlois answered back, "I want to rescue Uther just as much as the both of you but less we forget the animals of war are formidable enemies. The Phoenix, and Pegasus both can fly so we cannot use an attack during the day we must attack under the dark of night in order to have a chance to rescue Uther.
Gawain agreed that a night attack was the most cunning he would dismount his steed when they were close and lead his attack on foot to capture Helena. Garlois and Tarnish would hold back until Gawain gave the single to charge in as they faced these animals of war and rescued their fellow knight Uther. Just as they were about to enter Dartmoor Garlois heard hushed voices the men stopped as they listened. The Phoenix spoke, "Helena we must hurry get Uther to break open the prison and release the Manicore." The hard pyramid prison stood atop Mt. Dartmoor as the sun beams were upon it the glimmering pyramid shined like a rare jewel. Helena was just about to order Uther when Pegasus appeared. Helana assumed that Pegasus would persuade Merlin to join their quest when he returned without Merlin Helena questioned, "You have returned without Merlin where is he?" Where is Solana, The Lady of the Lake? Pegasus was out of breath trying to beat Merlin and the others before they lay siege to his plans as he was panting for air he muttered," Merlin is on his way but he is now our enemy. He will come soon to seek Uther so we must dash for he will be here soon. He has already sent a band of knights that ride here as we speak. Helena order

Uther to set free the Manicore so we can proceed to Mt. Olympus and destroy those vile gods for their treachery." Helena motioned to Uther beckoning him to come closer to the pyramid. Uther in his trace like state moved toward the massive triangular prison of the Manicore. Gawain and the others began to chant Merlin's name. Merlin heard their call. Merlin ran to Solana as they both were encompassed in protective sphere and were instantly transported to Gawain and the others. Gawain whispered to Merlin, They are about to release the Manicore from his mighty prison. We must act fast before they have the upper hand Garlios, Tarnish and myself have come up with a plan to attack. Merlin interjected, "this is end of the line. We must defeat the animals of war here and now. Dartmoor itself was Purple, heather clad moorland, with wide open space the rushing rivers, and obscure stone tors shape the landscape of Dartmoor. Gawain knew the best approach was to get the animals of war to the mires where they would have the advantage. Garlois watched onward as he saw that Uther was about to release the Manicore. Merlin acted quickly as he looked in the direction of Uther, Helena, Pegasus, and the Phoenix. His eyes started to glow a bright white as he concentrated his energy he called to the powers of the ancient as he chanted the spell to halt time itself, Merlin chanted "Time stand still I order you,
No minute pass until I'm through, doing what I need to do. Time stand still I order you. A shockwave of lighting cursed through Merlin's fingers toward Uther and the other. There fast action motion began to slow as they stopped. It was if time itself had stopped. The men looked to one another in sheer awe. Tarnish softly whispered, "By the god Merlin what have you done?"

Merlin replied, "I have bought us critical time to devise a plan to rescue Uther and put an end to Helena and the animals of war once and for all. Gawain explained the plan to Merlin and Solana all was set they would lure the animals of war to the marsh bogs of Dartmoor eerie forest lands. Gawain would set up clever traps within the forest. The marsh and bog land would be their fighting grounds. English men knew the dangers of the marsh. Dartmoors mires were known throughout the land to swallow man and animals alike. Garlois and Tarnish would await the signal from Gawain to attack. Gawain would lie in wait in the woods as the Merlin and Solana headed toward Uther to rid him of Helena evil spell. With the element of surprise. Uther would defy Helena orders to release the Manicore. Merlin and Solana then could leap into action lure the animals of war and Helena into the trap. Merlin approached Helana, Pegasus, and Phoenix with Solana at his side. Uther was to the right of them with Excalibur in hand ready to strike the pyramid prison of the Manicore to release onto the world once again. Merlin held Solana hand as they chanted the spell of banishment to free Uther from the clutches of Helena. The enchantment that Uther was under was very powerful. It took both Merlin and Solana power to break the spell over Uther. As they chanted in unison. "We summon forth my inner light to rid Uther of this foul sight.
Let their hold of force wither and depart from Uther's mind, and heart.
Let them now cease to be returning to their damned eternity. So we will it, so it be." Uther was freed at last Uther dropped Excalibur once he was freed from Helena's spell.

Merlin could not lift the tie halting spell just yet so he communicated with Uther telepathically as he describe the plan. Uther understood. Merlin and Solana readied themselves for battle. Gawain and the others set the traps and awaited the battle to commence. And deep within the eerier forest Gawain waited to strike down Helena. Merlin lifted his spell of status as Helena and the others began to move once more. Uther with Excalibur at the ready lead the strike. Uther ran towards Helena Pegasus flew down to investigate what was happening when he saw Merlin transform into the magi dragon. Solana held strong as the Phoenix moved in formation to strike at Uther. Solana called to the river bank as a great surge of water leaped to her Solana moved both her hands together over her head as she forced a wave of water to combat the phoenix's fire.

Uther running in the direction of Helena. Helena began to retreat within the eerie forest where Gawain lied in wait for her. Merlin and Pegasus battled within the skies. As the two of them clash together in a furry of talons clawing at one another. Merlin breathed fire synching Pegasus wings. Pegasus countered with a Zeus thunderbolt striking Merlin.

Gawain heard someone approach as he readied himself for the sneak attack. Gawain had to make sure it an enemy before he would lay siege. Helena moved rapidly through the forest trying to escape Uther racking her brain for the best way to attack Uther was formidable warrior and would not yield to a women. Helena stayed her course thinking she could out run Uther's advance. Gawain moved in as he saw Helena. Gawain lunged out of the brush to see Helena stood at the edge opposite. Gawain with his sword glinting in the late evening sun.

Uther on one side and Gawain on the other trapped Helena circling her with their two broadswords which hadn't spilled a lot of blood that day. Both blades looked almost pink in the dying light. They made brief eye contact with Helena who only smirked at them. Helena didn't want to admit the trap gave them edge, but it had.

Gawain and Uther were off. Helena shrieked at Uther all youth and lean muscle, leapt catlike from the ledge, waving Excalibur's blade in figure eights multiple times before touching down on the forest floor. Gawain cracked a smile. This time, he made sure to make eye contact. For a brief moment, he could see uncertainty in Helena's eyes. He felt grateful for the advantage.
Advancing. Advancing. Uther charged at Helena with the Excalibur's blade upheld, Helena dodged the first and met the second as she struck a powerful blow to Gawain's broadsword. The weight of the thing sent Helena back, back, back…but not far enough to knock the blade free of his hands.
Striking. This arcing shot sliced the fabric of Helena's dress at the midsection. It missed the flesh behind it by perhaps a centimeter. She staggered trying to regain her footing. Gawain swung.

His broadsword missed, though not close enough to eat fabric. Uther managed another smirk, this time at the spryness of Helena's dodge. Gawain had to admit it was impressive, but this time, the sight only made him angrier.

Swing. Swing. Swing. The first two missed badly, but the third, a back swing off the one before it, found flesh. The heavy broadsword ate through Helena as easily as air. The she dropped to a knee, tried to stand, and dropped again.
Gawain looked at Helena. The most vile bitch among the gods, yes, but the wound was not bad enough to kill her.. He raised his sword and smiled one last time, avoiding eye contact as he brought it down for the last strike as the blood cursed out of her. Uther still was not finished, with Excalibur he decapitated her holding her bloodied head in his hands he finally felt freedom.

Solana held the phoenix at bay Pegasus and Merlin battled in the skies Merlin sought retreat from Pegasus and headed into the forest. Solana did the same. The Phoenix and Pegasus on the advance followed them without caution. Once in the forest Merlin and Solana met up with Tarnish and Garlois you both know what you have to do. "Yes" Tarnish went first as he ran into the fray calling down the mighty Pegasus from the skies. Tarnish shouted, "Come down you vile beast I do not fear you fight me I seek your horn and I will beat you in this fight."

Pegasus was not one to be challenged in such a way he flew down to meet his aggressor and end his prideful taunting once and for all as he flew down. Pegasus hit Gawain's trip a wire that sent a massive net infused with magic that rendered Pegasus powerless. Pegasus struggled and fought trying to break free with no avail. The phoenix heard his cries for help and went to investigate as she did snares captured her as well both animals of war were once again captured.

# CHAPTER TEN
# THE TOMB OF THE ANIMALS OF WAR

Merlin knew what must be done to end this once and for all. He devised a plan to trap all the animals of war forever. Merlin called out "Uther you must aid me I have to shed my dragon skin forever. Uther was dumbfounded by Merlin request. "How can you help me with this Merlin? I do not understand what I can do." "Uther you must use Excalibur to pierce my dragon Hyde hurry there is no more time you must do it quickly.

Uther with fear in his eyes was bewildered why did Merlin want me to shed his skin? "Merlin why have you given me the task?"

Merlin looked to him with ache in his heart as he replied, "It is time Uther."

Uther you must shed my dragon skin. Hurry there is not time to waste do not worry about the pain as you shed my dragon skin hurry and do it now. Uther knew it must be done with his shaking hand he edged closer to Merlin as he transformed into the magi dragon. Uther pierced his skin very gently the green blood began to spill as he cut his skin the golden scales and ruby clusters fell to the lush green forest floor.

Tears streamed down Solana's face as her eyes redden watching her beloved endure pain as Uther continued to cut away at Merlin. As the dragon hide lay there, Merlin transformed back to his human form knowing that he would never be able to transform into the magi dragon again he wept.

Solana in shocked to see Excalibur covered in the green blood pooled at the tip of the sword. Merlin weeping, "All is well my love I have shed my skin of the dragon for good reason." Solana looked to Merlin with tear stained face as she uttered, "Why Merlin what have you shed your dragon skin for?"

"I had to do it so I could entomb the animals of war. You see Solana when you told me the tales of these beast. I knew there was only one way to hold them. I did not want to enslave them as the gods did. I wanted them to be together in harmony but I knew that harmony would not be here for they are not ordinary creatures of the forest they were created by the gods to strike fear in the hearts of men."

"I must place them in a new world where they live harmonious with one another. Don't you see it was the only way? I had an inspiration when you told your tales of ole. I knew that dragon skin was impenetrable. I will forge a book of beasts in this book I will create a land for the animals of war to live out their days together."

Solana replied, "Yes I see Merlin I understand now that we have your dragon skin what else do we need to forge this book of beasts."

"We must have, powerful magic of the ancients to forge this book. I must create the staff of power to forge the book. For once the book is forged I will use the staff of power to place the animals of war inside it forever."

Solana was overcome as she replied, "Staff of power what is the staff of power? How do we procure this staff of power?" Merlin with resolved on his faced answered, "The staff of power is a magical wooden staff it is made from the wood of the great oak , the incantations sealed within is delicate body.

At the head of the large staff is the jewel of time prism all three jewels of old will encapsulate above the staff yielding the power of the ancients. The staff would only be held by one of magi blood. It is also infused with the breath of the dragon.
Solana looked to Merlin with confused as she spoke, "Merlin how can we acquire these items the tree creatures are dead? The

jewels of time are scatted to the four winds. What about these incantations of which you speak and how are we to merge the staff in the dragons breathe for it to be infused? Merlin as growing frustrated with Solana and all her questions as he answered, "Yes it is true it will be a hard task ahead but we must do it and quickly for the dragon skin will soon decay." Garlois, Gawain and Tarnish were reminiscing together as Merlin, Solana, and Uther approached them.

Uther was the first to speak "Merlin thank you for freeing me from the clutches of the vile bitch Helena." Tarnish and the other stood next to Pegasus and the Phoenix. Merlin answered, "It was my pleasure but we don't have no time to revelry now. We must gather together once again in search of the jewels of time to build the staff of the ancients. It is the only way that we can truly encompass the animals of war in the book of the beasts."

The men stood in awe confused by Merlin's words. The animals of war were already trapped there was no need for this book of beasts. Garlois interjected, "I for one have fulfilled my quest in the aid of rescuing Uther. I have no time to follow in this force for the jewels of time. Ingrien is with child and needs me at her side. I bid you good day gents I am heading back to my lands." Garlois mounted up his horse and began to ride away.

Tarnish called out "Garlois do not leave us now there is still this matter of the animals of war. If we do not act now they will take over the world and enslave us mortals for their pleasure there will be no kingdom for you to rule."

Gawain interjected "I too want to return to my lands. I've grown tired of this but it is unfinished. These animals of war have been captured we must continue our course and end this threat once and for all." Uther bowed down at Merlin's feet as he spoke, "Merlin I believe in your cause. I owe you my life I pledge my sword and shield to your cause. Tell me how I can assist in your quest? Merlin replied, "We must return to Avalon once there we will begin now whose is with us. Tarnish Gawain nodded they too will join the cause.

Garlois stayed mounted on his horse. I am the black knight of Cornwall my duty is to my Kingdom and Ingrien. I wish you well good knights, but I am returning home. Garlois rode off in the distance. Gawain, Uther and Tarnish were in disbelief.

They could not believe that their once beloved companion would abandon them. Solana interjected, "The black knight has made his decision we must hurry back to Avalon so that we can start this new quest men so mount up." Uther, Tarnish, and Gawain mounted their horses as they rode towards Avalon. Solana and Merlin took to the skies as they levitated off the ground as they flew towards Avalon.

As they flew to the heavens Solana looked to Merlin as she stated," Merlin why are we going to Avalon there is no answers there? I search the catacombs for the whereabouts of the jewels of time. All I found was a scroll containing the legend of the jewels of time no more. Merlin sighed, "Solana the scroll that you speak of has a secret key embedded in the papyrus. Only one of great power can see the whereabouts of the jewels of time." Solana contemplated, **I am the Lady of Lake and considered herself one of great power of the scroll contains a secret key she should be able to see it.** "Merlin I am one who possess the power of the gods themselves why then could I not see this secret key on the papyrus?"

Merlin again was growing tired of all her questions as he groaned, "Solana you are a vessel for the goddess it is true that you have powers but you are not powerful enough the elders who hide the jewels of time did so that only one of great power who could harness that level of control over the jewels could see the secret key."

Tarnish, Uther and Gawain were dismayed that Garlois turn his back on them. Tarnish was hurt worst of all. Tarnish looked to the other two upset, "How could he do that? How could he ride off and leave us in a time of need? Gawain who was also unhappy at Garlois for his choice, It is beyond me how he could be so callus putting his own needs in front of his kingdoms like that. Garlois has made his choice and he will deal with consequences when this is over I assure you. Uther who bore feeling of jealousy for Garlois interjected, "I have no love loss for Garlois as you both know but do not make judgment on him for wanting to be with Ingrien she is with child now I am sure you myself and Tarnish would have done the same."

Tarnish begins to verbalize, "Maybe you are right Uther but I rescued Garlois. I brought him here he pledged his allegiance to me under oath I hold sacred for him to turn his back on me is an insult. Garlois has made me an enemy by his choice. I will have my retribution regardless of his need to be with his wife." Gawain agreed with Tarnish as he nodded. "I too feel hurt not only did he not invite myself or Tarnish to his wedding with Ingrien he now has turned his back on the very knights who need him most. Garlois will forever be an enemy of mine." Uther too was upset he was growing more and more angry as Gawain and Tarnish went on to tell him that they both had to go in search of him when they found that Uther had disappeared. That he then did not want to leave his kingdom. Only because of the oath did he depart and that was with a lot of persuading.

Uther was infuriated, "Ohh I see I who was his friend who fought side by side with him. I who gave away his one true love for him. I was not good enough to save. I understand more than ever why he was cursed my friends. I too agree with you Garlois is an enemy now. We will follow our quest with Merlin when we are finished brethren we will take satisfaction from Garlois are we agreed. Tarnish and Gawain nodded together as the answered in unison, "Yes Uther we agree." The knight rode long into the night as they reached the shores of Avalon once more.

Merlin and Solana followed as Solana parted the mists of Avalon the knights entered with Merlin. They raced to the catacombs of Avalon where Merlin searched for the scroll of the jewels of time. Solana where is the scroll I cannot find it. Solana concentrated on the scroll as her half-moon started to glow on her forehead a beam of light shot fourth leading to the whereabouts of the scroll. The light moved around the catacombs searching for the scroll centered on the scroll finding hidden among the many secrets of Avalon. Merlin followed the light to see the scroll at last. Merlin carefully picked up the scroll and began to read it.

As Merlin looked upon the scroll the letters started to change their sequence forming different words. It was the language of the ancients embedded in the scroll. Merlin read on to open the secret to the jewels of time one of great power must travel long distances once there seek the three alters of the goddess. Each alter will only surface when the great dragons breathe is evoked. Once the alter surfaces one of great power and true heart must speak the charm of making to the release the jewels of time. The moon stone is hidden in the highlands at the highest peak of the mountains known as Na Beanntan Dearga. The love stone is deep with the rushing waters of Lake Windmere. The blue sapphire is in the cavernous region of the tree creatures with in the heart of the tree of life. Merlin knew that the blue sapphire was already taken from the tree of life and embedded in Excalibur to help Helena release the animals of war. Merlin raced to the others formulating his plan to the last detail.

Merlin knew that he must possess all the jewels of time as well as the ruby dagger and the emerald necklace of the vampire for his plan to work. Merlin knew he would have to craft a staff of great power in order to create the book of beast and entomb the animals of war in harmony so they could be together. Merlin went to the great meeting hall as the knights and Solana waited for him. Merlin explained his plan to all of them.

"Uther since you already have the blue sapphire. I would ask that you return to Dartmoor and guard the animals of war. Gawain you must venture to the highlands with Solana. Once there Solana you must evoke the dragons breath to summon the alter of the goddess then you must recite the charm of making three times. The moon stone will reveal itself. Gawain you must then take the stone and bring it back here to Avalon. Tarnish and I will ride to Lake Windamere to retrieve the other stone.
First I must ask you Uther for Excalibur. Uther replied, "Yes Merlin you may have my sword."

Uther handed Excalibur to Merlin. Merlin took the mighty sword in hand as he spoke the words to release the blue sapphire from the sword. The sapphire was a glowing indigo blue triangle Merlin took a cloth and cover the magnificent stone. Merlin looked to Uther, "May the gods be with Uther"

Merlin handed back Excalibur to Uther all the men and Solana readied themselves for their journey. Gawain and Solana were the first to leave Uther followed then Tarnish and Merlin were the last to leave.

Gawain and Solana headed south to the highlands. Gawain was a little worried about this quest. He was not one to fool with the gods. Gawain feared the gods so he did not wait to anger them in any way.

Solana too was fearful of this quest. In reading of the scroll it told her that the jewels of time were powerful by themselves but when connected they would create a vortex thru time. Only one of great power could yield the jewels of time. She was also nervous about the charm of making.

Solana knew of the charm of making from the goddess it was a potent spell that only a few could wield without causing harm to themselves. Solana was told that only one of immense power and strength would be able to recite the charm of making.

Solana feared that once she started to chant the spell she would lose hers of in the incantation like some many others who tried the spell would infuse with the person as it took the life-force from the bearer of the spell they would be found devoid of life their bodies just dust.

Uther headed east toward Dartmoor. Uther was fixated on Ingrien growing more and more concerned about Ingrien. It was all he thought about she weighed on his mind. Uther was distraught at the fact she was with child. He knew what that meant she had made her decision. As he contemplated, **Why** *did she choose him? How could I let this happen? She is my one true love I don't understand this horrible fate the gods have chosen for me love is forever lost on me.* Uther rode to Dartmoor where Pegasus and the Phoenix were held imprisoned. Uther guarded the prisons as instructed by Merlin.

# CHAPTER ELEVEN
# THE LOVE STONE

Merlin and Tarnish headed to Bowness in search of the love stone. It was at the goddess temple of love. The stone was at the bottom of Lake Windmere. It was said that the goddess gave up her feelings of love to become immortal. She cast the love stone into Lake Windmere so she would not be tempted by her love. Lake Windmere was the deepest lake in the land.

Merlin and Tarnish raced to the town of Bowness which was on the out skirts of Lake Windmere. Tarnish was exhausted from the journey. He needed food, drink, and warm bed to rest. Merlin too needed a rest from the journey. They both dismounted and headed into the local inn. The inn was a small stone cottage with thatched roof. It was located in the heart of Bowness and surrounded by shops, and taverns. Bowness itself was a fishing village that sat on the shores of Lake Windmere. It was surrounded by hills and valleys of green lush lands. Lake Windmere was teeming with all kinds of wildlife from the beautiful swans, mallards, and gulls. In the center of the lake stood the goddess alter where it was rumored she had cut out her heart to become immortal. The goddess tossed her heart deep within Lake Windmere. Many villagers who are troubled by love seek out this alter and pray to the goddess to dispel their vile feeling of love.

Merlin and Tarnish enter the inn. Tarnish said, "We are in need of food, drink and lodging landlord can you obliged? The landlord responded, "I can squire as long as you have coin." Tarnish replied, "Yes landlord we have the coin." The landlord replied, "Fine then enter and I will round you up some of our foul for you and your friend to partake." Tarnish ordered, "Sir I would like bread and cheese with mulled wine now landlord. For dinner I fancy pheasant with stuffed roots and ale. My friend and I have been traveling for a long while and request bath and warm bed for the night.
Merlin was riddled with guilt he knew there was not time for this. "Tarnish we must hurry for I fear we are already losing precious time." Tarnish replied, "Yes Merlin I understand but we are but mortals and have limitations.

The landlord brought them two loaves of bread and some mulled. Tarnish was so ravenous that he engulfed the bread in one bite.

The mulled wine was devoured as well. Both men headed to rest from their long journey.

Merlin and Tarnish headed to the harbor to procure a vessel to take them to the goddess alter. There were a great many different ships in the harbor for hire. Long ships by the dozen sat on the dock. There were fishing vessels scattered about.

Tarnish arranged to get a small dinghy to cross the waters of Lake Windmere and gain access to the goddess alter. Tarnish was confused for he looked out in all directions across the water all he saw was water for miles there was no alter to be found. Tarnish and Merlin boarded the small dinghy. The boat itself was built of spruce strip planking and mortar, with one layer of glass cloth on the outside of the hull and ash frames and a partial second layer of spruce planking on the inside of the hull. Tarnish started rowed out the center of Lake Windmere where they began the search for the love stone of the goddess.

"Merlin all I see is water for miles where is the goddess alter?" Merlin started to think of the scroll from Avalon. **Each alter will only surface when the great dragons breathe is evoked. Once the alter surfaces one of great power and true heart must speak the charm of making to the release the jewels of time.**

Tarnish growing impatient shouted, "Merlin, Merlin can you hear me are you listening there is no alter here?" Merlin began to draw from the power within chanting as he rocked back and forth on the boat. Merlin raised his hands as bright lights shot threw his

fingertips onto the water. The light casts a shadow where the goddess alter lay dormant. Merlin looked to the heavens as he shouted, "Of the sky and of the ground,
May you cast your divine energies down.
Unto the light and unto the dark,
Holy Spirit, transcend into my heart.
Hear my pleas and ascend to earth,
I give you the portal to ascend to birth.
I invoke the dragons breath show me the alter of the goddess."

The water started to rumble as waves crashed down all the around the small boat in the water. A searing force of thick fog began to race toward Merlin and Tarnish it was the dragon's breath. Merlin was unmoved as Tarnish was overcome with fear his eyes widen at the spectacle of it all.

The dragons breath surrounded them searching out the goddess alter. As the dragons breathe emerged on the rectangular shape of light on top of the water's surface. The water started to dissipate as the alter ascended from the depths of lake Windmere. Tarnish rowed Merlin to the alter. Merlin looked upon the great stone tablet as it floated in the water. It had an image of the goddess carved in the center. Above her image was a mural that depicted the legend of goddess and the love stone. Merlin sensed the power of the love stone. Merlin sat in the middle of the alter as he began to focus his power on find the love stone.

Merlin concentrated all his thoughts on the love stone opening his mind's eye as he started to see the images of the goddess watching her play out the legend. The goddess took the secret dagger of the gods and pierced her chest as she cut out her heart. The goddess held the heart in her hands. I will never be controlled by this again. The goddess looked deep within the heart as she crystallized it forever encompassing her feeling.

The goddess need to cleanse herself of the heart so she threw it with all of her might into the deepest part of Lake Windmere. Merlin watched as the rosy pink stone of shimmering light fly like a flash as it cascaded into the murky depths of Lake Windmere. Merlin arose as he yelled for Tarnish, "I know where the heart is we must hurry there is no time to lose." Tarnish and Merlin rowed for hours. Finally they reached the sight of the love stone. Merlin could feel the love stone calling him it was at the bottom of Lake Windmere.

Merlin cast a spell of protection so he could enter the water. Tarnish was beside himself with fear. Merlin levitated down to the bottom of the lake where the love stone was embedded into the rocks below. Merlin remembered that he must chant the charm of making to release the love stone.

Merlin focused all his power as he started to chant the charm of making. He chanted, "anal nathrak, uthvas bethud, do che-ol di-enve" The love stone started to glow a rosy pink hue so bright that Tarnish who was still in the boat could see.

The rocks around the stone started to shatter as the love stone was free. Merlin reached out to grab the love stone as it fell in his hand it scorched his flesh. Merlin held the love stone enduring the soaring pain. Merlin elevated to the surface with stone in hand. Merlin entered the boat encompassing it trying to hold it blocking out the blinding light. Tarnish hurried as he grabbed the oars and rowed to shore. Merlin held the love stone in the palm of his hands. Once ashore Merlin raced to the horse he placed the love stone in a small black pouch.

Merlin then took herbs to protect the pouch as that the love stone would not burn threw it. Merlin motioned to Tarnish, "We must journey to the ancient forest of Isleham to gain the wood for the staff of power. Then hurry back to Avalon with the love stone. "Yes Merlin" both men mounted their horses riding back toward Avalon.

Merlin and Tarnish headed to the ancient forest of Isleham. It was their only hope to find the sacred wood of the great oak the last surviving member of the tree creatures. Merlin was feeling the effects of the love stone his hands burned, the pain was unbearable it was all he could do to hold the reins on his horse Tarnish could see Merlin was in pain. "Merlin perhaps we should stop at the nearby village their maybe an herbalist there that can help with your aliment." Merlin was trying to fightback the tears as he muttered, "Yes I cannot go on like this Tarnish let us find and herbalist in the nearby village." Tarnish and Merlin rode throughout the village in search of an herbalist on the edge of the village was a small stone cottage with a thatch roof. There was a sign hanging above the door. Tarnish dismounted his horse to take a closer look the sign. The sign was burned into the wood the black emblem was a dragon that was caught between a diamond and a pyramid. Yes it the sign of a healer Tarnish announced Merlin hurry there is a healer here. Merlin rode up to the cottage he dismounted his horse very carefully as the pain throbbed through his hands. Tarnish knocked on the small arched door. Tarnish explains, " We are in need of a healer for my friend he is badly wounded Healer are you here?" There was a faint raspy voice, "Yes come in" Tarnish and Merlin entered the dark entryway almost completely pitch black except for the faint light of one candle inside were shelves filled with vials and bottles of mixtures to the left and right the aroma was fragment with herbs of all kind peppermint, lavender, and dill weed were the most prevalent. The floor creaked as a little meek old man entered the room "You knights are in need of my services" Tarnish tried to make out the man expression as he squinted to see his small shape. Yes you see healer my friend hands were badly burned by….. Tarnish knew that there were among strangers so he would have to improvise what had happened to Merlin to avoid suspension horribly burned."

"I see knight by what was your friend burned by?" Tarnish spoke out quickly "by the coals in the fire." The healer knew that Tarnish was not be at all truthful to him but he needed coins so he did not question him further about the reason for his friends injury. The healer replied, "Have your friend come in so that I can examine these burns on his hands." Merlin covered his face with a hood trying to conceal his identity Merlin held out his hand the charred skin with red blisters the deep burns marks embedded in his palms. The healer looked at his wounds with care. It is trickery you bring to my house those burns are not caused by fire knight those burns were cause by powerful magic!!! The healer exclaimed as he threw up his hands in disgust for the knight. "I can heal your friend but I must know the true reason for these burn on his palms in order to make the right mixture. Now what say you knight as the small man pointed his finger in Tarnish direction. What cause these wounds? The healer demanded. Tarnish knew he had to reveal the real reason for Merlin's wounds as he looked to Merlin before he spoke. Merlin nodded as Tarnish began to explain Healer it is true that these wounds were not cause by coals in the fire they were caused by the love stone of the goddess. Before Tarnish could finish the healers eyes widen with sure terror as his voice trembled, "You have the lover stone of the goddess you must be powerful necromancer indeed to yield such power only one of the highest skills would dare to attempt such a fate like Merlin" The healer slapped his head "Merlin is that you?" Merlin who was overcome with pain was starting to become ill-tempered as he shout Yes now that you have solved the riddle can you heal my wounds or not? Oh yes right away I will make the potion now the healer hurried about the small hovel searching for his herbs as he mixed them together in such a fashion a pitch of this a dash of that now where is the bloody aloe yes two drops of dried ginger root. Tarnish and Merlin stood and watch the display of sure delight as the mad healer finished his work. The healer poured all the mixture into a giant caldron and placed under the small hearth "Now where is my flint I know I put it right here last night. Yes now I remember I lit the candle as you came in."

The healer ran to the other room grabbed the flint as he lit the logs under the caldron. The caldron started to bubble as hues of crimson and gold flashed "Yes it coming together nicely it will soon be finished." Tarnish and Merlin were confused by the healer's method how was this boiling hot liquid to heal Merlin's burned hands both men stood puzzled.

  The healer had a huge ladle that he used to pour the mixture into a frozen vial as the hot liquid cooled Merlin screamed out in pain AHHH. The healer ran to him with the frozen vial in hand as he pour out just two drops Merlin I am sorry to tell you but the love stone had marked you anytime you pine for your lady love the pain in your palms will increase until you are with your lady love the sauce I have prepared will dull the pain only for a short while so use it sparingly as you have a limited supply. Now for my coin knight. Tarnish paid the healer as Merlin mounted his horse Tarnish did the same as they rode to Isleham. Merlin and Tarnish rode for days and finally they arrived on the edge of the woods. It was breathtaking as the upper limb of the sun disappears below the horizon the brilliance of Mother Nature becomes apparent. To the left across the lake low-lying hills clouds crawl upward across the horizon. In front of them covered by a countless trees, this lone secluded forest. To the right of Merlin and Tarnish the hills gradually turn to mountains.
  A wide vast Oak stand before them. The Oak's finger-like branches delicately reach down toward the lake, trying to touch the water. High above them, moisture laden clouds span out over the mountain tops, resembling a magenta colored quilt. Facing them a broadening division in the clouds crests with a final effort

to avoid succumbing to the shroud of night. The ever present forests balances upon the water's edge, reflecting a perfect vision of its unblemished counterpart. It is a mirrored understatement of nature's true beauty.

# CHAPTER TWELVE
# LUCIFER'S BLUEPRINT

Desmoria/Ezerbeth was running out of time Lucifer was gearing up to drag her back to Hellfire. Lucifer knew that she was building her blood supply tempting maidens throughout the kingdom. She collected all the maidens and now she had started dipping her fangs into regal families the ladies of the court have recently gone missing bodies are piling up.

Whispers scoured the kingdom of her involvement with black magic rumors were she was a witch or worse.
Desmoria/Ezerbeth was losing favor with her people.　She had

taken up with the druids as she focused her attentions on black magic. Lucifer has watched and waited.

She had made so many enemies but the most vile enemy was Thorzo her husband's comrade in arms as well as her own cousin. After Desmoria/Ezerbeth had her husband Frenic murdered Thorzo plotted his revenge waited for the right time to strike. Desmoria/Ezerbeth was royalty any accusation made would have to be supported by strong evidence or the accuser would face sure death without hesitation.

He treaded lightly waiting for Desmoria/Ezerbeth to make a fatal mistake. She was a very shrewd women who was very caution not to draw attention to herself. She would not be careless to make a mistake. Desmoria/Ezerbeth was growing desperate she knew that her time on Earth would be finished if she did not do something soon.

Lucifer started his campaign to destroy her. Lucifer engaged Thorzo in a dream. Lucifer used his powers of the subconscious to weave into Thorzo dream. Lucifer painted a picture of the heinous acts Desmoria/Ezerbeth committed the vile debauchery that these peasant girls suffered made Thorzo's skin crawl and his sleeping body broke out in to a cold sweat.

Lucifer was not done as he push the threshold of Thorzo to the brink when he showed how Desmoria/Ezerbeth murdered her own son in a brutal act of sacrifice to the Devil. Still images of Desmoria/Ezerbeth lair and torture chamber awaited him. The room was dark and dank covered all in black. Druids casting dark magic chanting as they would spilling innocent blood from maidens chained to the wall slashing their throat as they collected the blood.

 In the center of the room was a large white bath made of the finest white marble. Inside the bath was a crimson pool of blood as the druids pour more fresh blood in Desmoria/Ezerbeth would drink of the blood as it absorbed into her body. As she bathed in the blood of the innocent maidens her fangs protruded she immersed herself fully in the bath. She drank of the blood emptying the bath fully. Not wasting a single drop she stood naked covered in blood as she licked herself clean.

Thorzo thrash violently in his bed chamber back and forth tossing and turning as he witnessed all this horrors unfold before his very eyes. As the fear began to intensify his skin turn pure white. Thorzo awoke frighten beyond words shaking with fear.

Lucifer sent whispers into his minds eye he had to act and do it now before the whole of the kingdom was succumb to Desmoria/Ezerbeth. The images from the dream so fresh on his mind. **I must act quickly before it is too late. If there is breath in my body I swear to rid this evil from our lands. Desmoria/Ezerbeth was a vile creature of dark magic. She is a vicious vampire who feeds on human flesh. The arrogance of her to bath in the blood of all those maidens as she drank her bath, how vile this demon women is the image of her haughts** my very soul as she stood naked covered in blood I must stop her I must warn the King.

Thorzo saddled his horse as he rode to see the king. He reached the castle as he dismounted and approached the mighty keep gate the knights were on waiting, "who goes there state your business." It is I, Thorzo I seek audience with the king on a vital matter to discuss with him. I implore you let me pass. The knights held their ground as they summoned the page tell the Kings valet that Thorzo request an audience.

The page hurries into the main hall of the castle. Down the hallway to the throne room The King was at court the page burst into the throne room looking for the King's valet The page see the valet out of the corner of his eye as he motioned the valet to come to him. His hand beckoning the valet.

The valet goes to the page irritated in his manner, "Well what is it page? Why are you causing such a spectacle in front of the whole court out with it boy."

The page was out of breath from running, "I.... mean.... no offense but, the knights have a Lord requesting audience with the King to discuss a vital matter of importance." The valet's eyes rolled with his disgust for the pages manners, "Alright I will see if the King will grant this Lord audience you wait here and do not move a muscle."

The valet headed back to the kings side ever so smoothly trying to not draw attention from the court. The valet approach the King as he explained the situation to the King. The valet waited for the King to respond as he was interest by one of the fair ladies of the court who was flirting with him as she feed him grapes. "Yes I will see this Lord show him to the study and I will be there in a moment."

The valet nodded to the page who was awaiting his reply. The page left the throne room and headed back to the tower. The knights were perch high above in the tower watching the castle gates the page ran up the winding steps. "The…... King…... Grants the count audience you are you show him to the Kings study."

The knights open the massive gate as Thorzo entered the kingdom the page was there to meet him as he bowed to the ground "sir come with me I will take you to the Kings study." Thorzo dismounted his steed the page whisked him into the castle through the entryway to a large hall down a corridor to the Kings study.

Thorzo waited for the King all the while the horrible images from his dreams running through his mind so vivid Desmoria/Ezerbeth was a monster attacking commoners and royals alike all to feed her bloodlust. So horrific that he was petrified when the King arrived. The King convened the court and headed for his study.

What the King witnessed sent his blood cold. As he looked upon Thorzo his face colorless with fear in his widen eyes. "My good count what frightens you so please tell me to ease your pain I will promise you sanctuary."

Thorzo bowed, "Your highness I have grave news for you Desmoria/Ezerbeth has taken up with the druids she is using black magic your grace. Many say she is ......... The King was intent on every word that Thorzo utter, "Yes it is alright tell me count what is she?"

Thorzo with fear is his eyes shouted, "A VAMPIRE her subjects fear her your highness. Her inner circle has expressed to me that she worships the devil"

The King was mortified to hear these things terrible accusations against his family. The King thought for a moment as he clasp his chin, "I hear your accusation but Thorzo do you have proof of this to attest that what you are saying is true."
Thorzo did not have any physical evidence to back up his claim so he had to have the King agree to give him a vassal of men to be witness to all his statements. "Yes King I have the proof if you would grant me with a vassal of men you trust I will show the horrors on which I speak. Once they have seen with their own eyes I would ask that you allow those men to imprison Ezerbeth for trial and kill all who follow her. If we could go now and surprise her. Ezerbeth would not have time to build her defenses."

The King had a soft place in his heart for the hardships she faced at the loss of her husband. The agony she faced as her only son was murdered by the Turks. Such a tragic life for her. The King knew of the rumors that were spreading of her throughout the kingdom. He knew there was no choice he must for the court and Kingdom get to the bottom of this once and for all.

"Yes I will grant your request Thorzo. I will give you a vassal of men to serve as witness. I will also entrust you with two clerics to witness to Ezerbeth perhaps they can reach out to her. Of course I do not believe this of Ezerbeth. Thorzo you mark my words if your claim is unfounded I will have you beheaded."

Thorzo replied, "Your Grace I would expect nothing less of you. I would like to leave as soon as possible due to the severity of my claim I will be outside awaiting your men my King." He turned to the King and bowed as he was shown out by the page.

The vassals of men joined Thorzo as they headed back to Csejte castle. The clerics rode behind the knights. Both the clerics were amazed at the charges that Count Palentine claimed. They were unsure that they could bring her back from the depths of the darkness. If she indeed was as Count Palentine had stated a vampire could it be so. They both thought these accusation were false as they rode on towards Csejte castle. The older of the two clerics was a bishop who was appointed by the Pope to watch over the land and bring the lord to the faithful. He was a man of a humble home who was a monk that was granted priesthood at a young age as his will for the lord moved him ever forward he was given vancanency over the land and named bishop.

His companion was a peasant of the church who was inducted into the clergy by the bishop he was a priest. "Yes bishop I was taught to believe that the vampire was a myth surely there has been some sort of mistake." The bishop assured his young priest with a shake of his head, "No there is no mistake my young priest Count Palentine stated that he had it on the highest authority that Ezerbeth was a vampire who feeds on the blood of the innocent virgin maidens of this land. It is rumored that she worships the devil within the castle walls."

The young priest was horrified to hear such things from the bishop as his eyes filled with fear he muttered, "No bishop you don't mean it." The bishop sensed the fear in his young companion's voice as he replied, "Yes my novice that is what Count Palentine has stated in his claim. We must hurry and catch up with the knights for we are almost upon Csejte castle." The knights picked up speed

"Surely he would wait for day light to approach the castle right bishop?" the priest replied. The bishop had no doubt in his mind that the determined Count Palentine would do just that. "Yes I believe that he will so be ready my young priest. The Count burst through the gates at the castle. The guards were on the offensive.

The battle was fierce as swords clashed. The vassal of knights cut down the guards quickly they stormed onward through the courtyard marching through the entryway of the castle where a line of highly skilled men awaited their attack.
The vassal of men fought through the line. The Count shouts toward the men, "This way men hurry." The clerics followed the consulate off carriage headed toward the sacred lair of Ezerbeth. The Count led them down the hall where large taperisties and family portrait of the royal family hung on the wall to conceal a passageway. Count Palientine thought, *"This is just like my dream."*

The passage was pitch black one of the clerics grabbed a torch off the wall to light their way. The passage was vile with the smell of rotten meat and excrement. The knights held their breath to avoid the stench. The men and clerics came upon the druids in the mists of a ritual. The clerics were mortified at the sight of such unspeakable events.

The knights rounded up the druids without a fight. The Count led them through the druids alter toward the center of the room where Ezerbeth sat bathing herself in a pool of blood Ezerbeth arched her back as she levitated into the air trying to escape. The knights were awe stricken at the sight of this. The leader of the knights asked, "How are we to catch this flying demon?" Count Palentine took the holy water from the bishop he doused Ezerbeth with the holy water which caused her to lose control as she fell to the floor.

The knights rushed to capture her before she had time to defend herself. She tried with all her might to push through the knights but to no avail. "Count Palentine what is the meaning of this I am one of royal family." Count Palentine replied, "I am here by order of the King. Ezerbeth was livid as she shouted, "I am not governed under any law Count Palentine."

Count Palentine was overjoyed at her displayed with a cocked smile he replied, "The kings has asked that the bishop and the priest witness your crimes Ezerbeth now knights throw her into the dungeon to await her trail. As for the rest of rabble kill them so they will not darken this kingdom with their black magic any longer." The knights shackled the druids one by one as they stood in a lined row across the wall the knight took out their swords and slit the throats of the druids as their black blood seeped out of their dismember bodies the knights collected the heads of all the druids as they staked them on posts for displayed out in front of the castle to show the court that black magic was not to be tolerated by the king.

Ezerbeth was taken to the dungeon to await her trial the clerics followed trying to witness to her. Both the clerics began to witness saying in unison, "You must repent your sins ask Jehovah to forgive your wickedness. Bask in the waters of the divine the cleric threw holy water on Ezerbeth Jehovah is the one true god what say you Ezerbeth? Do you repent your sins? "

Ezerbeth skin started to burn when the holy water hit her alabaster skin. She knew she was in a terrible mess she had nowhere to turn but to Lucifer. She grasp her amulet calling to Lucifer summoning him to come to her aid. Lucifer heard her calls he knew she was locked up in cell so he appeared as a small snake as he slithered on the ground hissing, "Yes Desmoria/Ezerbeth you summoned me."

Desmoria/ Ezerbeth spoke in a hushed tone, "You have to help me Lucifer. I am in trouble I was trying to acquire Merlin for you but he has disappeared. Now I have been imprisoned by the king. I am facing trial Lucifer please help me I am begging you."

Lucifer was delighted by her plight he arranged it. The small scaly snake slithered closer to Desmoria/Ezerbeth replying, "As you know I have given ample time to turn Merlin. All the while I watched as you squandered that time on yourself. Merlin returned to his time where he is right now. Merlin is working towards enslaving the animals of war. Soon he will become more powerful than most of the gods. Merlin is creating the staff of power right now….."

Desmoria/Ezerbeth interjected, "Please Lucifer transport me to the past. I will turn Merlin I have built up my defenses. I have the love spell that will not fail only do so now. Once Merlin falls in love with me he will do whatever I wish Please Lucifer I beg you!!!"

Lucifer grew tired of her pleas as he exclaimed, "I could help you or I could wait and take you back to Hellfire. I believe I will wait. I will let you face your fate. Desmoria/Ezerbeth was in complete disarray as she heard Lucifer, "But you promised me Lucifer I still have one more favor left."

Lucifer stated, "Tis true but I am not known for being a trustworthy god. I lack honesty No I believe it is in my best interests to let you face your fate I believe I will enjoy your suffering by the hands of these barbarians yes I think that is the best idea." Desmoria/Ezerabeth was beyond livid she was furious as she declared, "HOW Dare you betray me Lucifer. You will regret this moment."

Lucifer thought it laughable that she would dare to threaten a god. He laughed aloud, "Ha ha you jest madam I regret nothing. If I were you I would worry more about your current circumstances and less of your rage right now Lucifer disappeared.

The clerics were shouting out scriptures begging Ezerbeth to repent her sins. She was still infuriated she hissed at the clerics showing her fangs to scare the clerics. The clerics were not deterred as they shouted, "By order of the King repent your sins accept Jehovah as your God."

She knew her situation was dire so the best thing for her to do was repent her sins showing good faith to her cousin the King. She kneeled to the floor Yes I repent my sins I praise Jehovah I accept Jehovah as god all mighty forgive me. Forgive me I was led astray by the druids they placed me under this curse they played on my sympathy after my sons was murdered by the Turks. The druids told me they could find the killer of my son. I was filled with anger and grief. I did not use my better judgment Please forgive me Jehovah.

The clerics were overjoyed to see Ezerbeth repent they opened the dungeon to release the princess that was their fatal mistake. The clerics entered the dungeon to embrace Ezerbeth. As the Bishop moved towards her she set her attack. She grabbed him by the arm and threw him across the room as his head hit the stone wall he was knocked out.

The priest could not believe what had just happened. He became paralyzed with shock. She took the holy water and the cross off of the priest and threw them to the ground. She drove her fangs deep within his flesh blood spattered everywhere wiping her mouth as she drained the priest of his life force. The lifeless body of the priest fell to the dungeon floor.

Ezerbeth/ Desmoria moved toward the bishop she was going to enjoy this. The bishop lay there. She tore at his flesh mutilating him to this unrecognizable figure. She lunged her fangs deep within his chest Ezerbeth/ Desmoria lingered enjoying each drop of blood as if it were a fine vintage of wine savoring it slowly. The bishop's blood was intoxicating she wanted to revel in it.

Unfortunately she had to hurry. She drained all of his blood as his white corpse lay on the ground. She knew that the knights were fortifying the castle so she would have to make herself unseen. She knew of only one enchantment that could make her hidden. She grasp her amulet as she chanted

"Unseen to the eye obvious to the touch in its cold uncomfortableness I call onto thee if you hear this plea give me the gift of invisibility it is my will so it be." As she chanted the incantation her body started to disappear from sight. First her hand dissipated, then her torso, next her legs until she was completely invisible.

She went in search of the druids to find their dismembered bodies in shackles against the wall. Their heads were nowhere to be found.

Ezerbeth/Desmoria already knew their fate. She knew that the King would make an example of their heads to show the court his feelings on black magic. She was beside herself now that the druids are dead who would help her return to the past.

She must make Merlin fall in love with her. She had to prevent him from enslaving the animals of war. As well as making the staff of power. Lucifer was going to damn her forever in hellfire if she did not move quickly. She considered, *I cannot let Lucifer win I must think come now there must be something. Aha I have it I must find Dorotya Semtész. Dorotya ran off just a week ago today. That bitch must have had a vision of these events and fled for her own safety. It is just like Dorotya to think of herself. I must find her she is my only hope to find Merlin and move forward with my plans.*

## CHAPTER THIRTEEN
## SOLANA RETRIEVES THE MOONSTONE

Gawain and Solana traveled to the highlands. It was bitter cold as they approached the snow covered hills everything was covered in ice as he evergreens glistened against the sunlight it looked as if the land was cover in diamond luster. Gawain packed furs with heavy boots for their journey but even with his preparation the brutal north wind left them chilled to the bone. What do you say lass should we break camp with chattering teeth Solana replied Yes build a fire I am freezing. Gawain dismounted his steed in search of limbs to build a fire Solana delved into her powers of the elements as she chanted a spell to make the wind blow the snow away so that Gawain could retrieve the dead limbs and branches. Solana moved her hands in a swaying motion creating small blast of wind moving the snow into large piles as she point her hand to the ground rounded stones appeared in a large circle in the center of the harden ground creating a fire pit. Gawain stacked all the limbs and branches into a triangle in the middle of the fire pit. He headed to his horse in his saddle bag was a small piece of flint. Gawain struck the flint against one of the stones in the fire pit sending sparks onto the wood as the fire started to burn slow at first then as the larger limbs caught they had a cozy fire. The warmth of the fire melted the cold from their bodies. Gawain questioned, "Lass are you warm enough now?" Solana who was now beginning to feel her toes again professed, "Yes Gawain I am quite warm now I had no idea it would be this cold here." Gawain affirmed, Aye lass the highlands are in winter always because Zeus built them so high in the mountains even in the summer it still remains cold most of the mountains have snow year round. Solana was astonished to learn about the highlands as she answered back, I never knew that Gawain I do know that we still have a long way to travel to reach the highest peak of the highlands tomorrow so I bid you good night Gawain. Gawain too knew it was still a long journey as he replied "Yes lass we still have a long way to go up the mountain. Good night Lady of the Lake may the gods watch over and protect us on our quest. Gawain too started to fall asleep. Solana could not rest she was worried about her task ahead. The charm of making was not a spell for a novice. Those who attempted the spell who were not ready perished under its power. Solana feared that she would suffer that fate as well. Over and over in her mind she imagined herself reciting the charm of making as she loses control the spell itself would possess her. She witnessed the spell take her body over and age her to dust. Solana needed reassurance she concentrated on Merlin he could ease her worries. Solana tapped deep within her heart to their love bond call out to Merlin. "Merlin can you hear me Merlin my love are you there."

Merlin and Tarnish were just outside the ancient forest Merlin cried out in pain the blood curling scream awoke Tarnish from a sound sleep, Merlin what is it that pains you so, Merlin shouted my hands my hands Merlin's hand were red hot Tarnish raced to the horses to get the vial of healing mixture here Merlin Tarnish poured two drops into each of Merlin's hands which soothed his pain to a dull ache. He could Solana's voice Merlin can you hear me where are you? Merlin still feeling the effects of the suave whispered yes beloved please speak quietly Solana could sense something amiss with Merlin as she questioned, Merlin what is the matter? Merlin in hushed tones spoke softly "The love stone has some unexpected after effects. Please Solana only contact me if you are in grave danger. I am sorry dear heart what troubles you?" Solana replied, "I am sorry Merlin but I am in doubt I do not believe I can do this task you have given me. I am not strong enough to recite the charm of making. I fear my demise is close at hand Merlin." Merlin could sense Solana's reluctance she knew that he needed to reassure her. Merlin answered back, "Solana my love you are The Lady of the Lake vessel to the goddess. You are of magi blood I believe in you I know you can do it if I did not believe in you I would have not given you this task Solana."

She was confident now about her task Solana was renewed She thanked Merlin for his faith in her. Merlin wanted to know if they were close to the moon stone because he did not want Solana to suffer the same fate as himself as he questioned, "Are you close to the moonstone?" She replied yes Merlin we are close we should have it by nightfall. He warned Solana, "Do not try to handle the moon stone with your bear hands use the pouch!" Solana listened to Merlin warning affirmed, Yes Merlin I will and again thanks for believing in me I will see you soon my love may the gods be with you. Merlin confirmed, and also be with you dearest.

Solana drifted off to sleep. Gawain awoke alone The Lady of the Lake had already arisen. She went foraging for food for break feast. She found some wild berries honeycomb, thistle root, also she managed to catch some small game. Solana returned to Gawain who was stretching trying to wake to the morn. Ah lass you have returned now where did you venture off too? Solana was proud of her merger forging skills as she took the small cauldron from her saddle bag. I went in search of some food to fill our bellies Gawain. Pray due tell Lady of the lake what are we going to dine on this morn. Solana felt great accomplishment as she told of her morning forging I found these berries on the hillside to the left of us they were on a small vine I followed that lead me to dying evergreen. Low and behold there in the tree was an abandon honeycomb. Onward I venture as I saw a bright purple flower atop a thistle   plan. When I heard this small chirp I followed the sound to a pheasant's nest where I found two eggs as I grabbed the eggs the mother pheasant started to attack me. I grabbed ahold of the pheasant neck and broke it on the spot. Gawain was so enticed with Solana story when he heard that she had not only gathered berries and thistle  but she had eggs and a pheasant he licked his lips Lass how'd you know I liked thistle root? Solana replied I guess I was just lucky. Gawain thrilled stated, "by the gods Solana if you were not spoken for I would ask for your hand what a women." Solana blushed enough of your charm Gawain. We must hurry up so eat. We need to get the moon stone before nightfall. Aye lass you are right. Solana cooked the eggs as the pheasant and thistle root stewed in the cauldron she took the berries and honeycomb and placed them in the saddle bags for later. Gawain and Solana ate until their hearts content. They mounted their horse and headed up the mountain. The climb was grueling every muscle in their body's ached when they reached the top Solana could feel the goddess present. The half-moon on her forehead began to glow. Her half-moon shout out a light beam directly over the moonstone. Gawain froze with fear as he witnessed the power of The Lady of the Lake. That must be where the alter is lass come lets go Yes Gawain I feel the goddess  presents here it's  now or never Solana headed to the alter site. She stood on the edge of the ridge mountain as she began to recite the charm of making chanting the words of the mountain started to quake and rumble a huge fisher of ground from the earth started to ride up into the air. The goddess alter was atop the massive fisher. Solana was too weak to retrieve the moon stone Gawain approached the goddess alter to retrieve the moonstone. Solana remembered Merlin's warning about retrieving the moonstone. She shouted "Gawain no wait you must use the magic pouch to retrieve the moon stone do not touch it with your bare hands." Gawain turned on his heels toward the horse in a dead run grabbing the magic pouch. He approached the alter again. Gawain looked upon the moon stone for the first time, the moon stone was mesmerizing it was a soft shade of pale blue almost white there was an icy fog that surrounded the moonstone. It was frozen to the alter of the goddess. Gawain took out his mighty broadsword and with the brunt hilt of his massive sword he struck the moon stone dislodging it from the goddess's alter.

Gawain took the pouch and covered the moonstone. Gawain closed the pouch and grab the precious stone as he retrieved it from the goddess's alter. Gawain exclaimed I have it let us take our leave of this place let go back to Avalon Solana. Solana took on the edge of the mountain exhausted as she agreed with Gawain. I need you to assist me please I am too weak to mount my horse myself. Aye Lass but let us go away now. Gawain took the moon stone back to his horse and placed it in the saddle bag. He ran back to Solana as he lift her in his giant arms and placed her gently on her horse. Gawain mount his horse and the rode toward Avalon. As they rode off into the distance the colossal mountain peak started to fold into itself the huge fisher upon which stood the goddess's alter started to crumble first then the mountain collapse into a giant crater. As the aftershock was sent throughout the highlands. The ground trembled beneath the horse's hooves spooking them into a panic as they reared up and bolted through the village trying to gain their footing. Solana held on with all her might as her horse was swiftly moving everything was a faint blur. Gawain right beside her was trying to slow both the horses. As He held his horse with one on the reins and

Solana's horse with other. Finally Gawain managed to slow them down enough to halt them both.


Merlin and Tarnish headed to the woods in search of the great oak. Merlin knew the great oak was a living creature. It was rumored throughout the land that the great oak was elusive. Tarnish was growing tired of all this riding as he questioned, "Merlin what are we looking for? All I see is yet another wood there is nothing special here just trees grass just any other forest in the land." Merlin knew that Tarnish was growing weary of all this travel but he sensed something in this forest. He could not quite put his finger on the trees were young but he sensed something very old here. Merlin answered back, You are mistaken my friend it's true that we are in a wood but stop looking with your eyes and feel the trees they may look like ordinary young trees but these trees are as old as time itself Merlin brushed his hand against the luscious ash wood bark. Do you see the colossal growth of this Ash as it towers into the air over looking fields and valleys? The beauty of the floral bouquet among the majesty. Enjoy the true wonderment of nature. Tarnish was still annoyed replied, "You enjoy the wonderment I want to find this bloody great oak so we can return to Avalon." Just as Tarnish finished his statement a loud ominous voice professed his displeasure in Tarnish's words. You dare not enjoy the gifts that are given to you well here mortal feel my wrath. Acorns came shooting through the air aimed at Tarnish vines came up from the ground winding around his feet. Tarnish was unable to move as an on salute of branches started to whip him for his insolence. Merlin looked to see his friend in dire trouble he called out, "Oh great oak please spear my dim whited companion for he is grown tired of our long journey he means no disrespect." The great oak spoke once more, "I believe he has learned his lesson well my brother's rest now." Merlin watched as the vines retreated back into the ground and the branches stop whipping Tarnish. Merlin did not want to lose contact with the great oak so he quickly called out Great Oak you have created a beautiful utopia within the land. I am Merlin of Avalon I come to your forest for your aid. The Great Oak has heard of the young necromancer Merlin he was intrigued. The great oak bellowed, "Merlin of Avalon come closer so that I may look upon you." Merlin moved forward toward the voice deep within the forest stood the biggest tree Merlin had ever laid his eyes upon the oak stood 200 foot into the air. Four massive limbs held the millions of leaves and branches that towered over the landscape. Merlin you are a magi from Avalon I sense you power is strong. Merlin declared "I am magi great oak"

The great oak questioned, "Why have you brought a man of Adam in our mist? Merlin answered back, "He is on a quest of great importance with me great oak He is true of heart and sometimes strong willed but he means no harm." The great oak was growing more and more interested in why Merlin sought him out. The great oak replied, I see you wear the robes of your ancestors Merlin you are an old soul in a young body you have recently shed your dragons skin to become magi why pray tell? Merlin did not realize the great oak was so in tune with the magi as he replied, Yes Great oak I am in need of your aid in our quest to reunite the animals of war. Great oak I know you feel the imbalance of the power right now Helena wanted to wage war on the gods for her own vengeance to the tree creatures but she brought that upon her people when she tried to enslave the Golden Hind as a result of her folly the goddess sent the ultimate punishment. Killing the tree creatures and making her watch unable to move. I understand her rage oh great oak but it was her who caused the end of the tree creatures not the gods." Yes Merlin I too have sensed the unrest within the land but how can I aid you? Great Oak what I ask of you is for the good of all remember that well what do you want of me Merlin I want one of your branches. You ask a great sacrifice indeed in order to protect the earth and the gods what will I receive in return for such a valuable token Merlin had nothing to offer the great oak Tarnish spoke up I will pledge my alliance to you great oak I will protect your magnificent forest for all my life this I swear. By my blood I make it so Tarnish took out his dagger and sliced his flesh as the drops of blood spilled onto the forest floor the pack was forever bound.  The great oak was overwhelmed with gratitude as he interjected, "I am awe struck this is a great gift you have given a man of Adam gives himself to the forest I am deeply moved.  I will grant your request for one of my branches. The Great Oak shook his canopy as the massive limbs started to sway a huge branch severed crashing toward the ground Merlin caught the branch in midair with and incantation. The Branch levitated as it was slowly dropped to the forest floor. The Great Oak spoke once more I trust this to you necromancer use it with care Merlin. He knew the great sacrifice it was for the Great Oak to part with just one branch he turn to the great oak and bowed Yes you have my word as a magi I will only use it for the good of the land. Tarnish and Merlin headed out of the forest towards Avalon.

Uther was with the animals of war thinking constantly about the Lady Ingrien, **How he longed to see her. He wanted to be with her as her husband to share in her joy. To be by her side was all he could think about. Now he was plagued with the thoughts of her with Garlois. She was having his baby how she could turn her back on our love. What was she thinking when she gave herself so willing to him? Rage was fueling his every thought now he was short tempered. My heart urns for her my body aches for her what can I do. I must focus on my task I must guard the animals of war until Merlin returns.** Pegasus and the Phoenix were in stasis unable to move just watching there surrounding every changing in front of their eyes. Like they were on the outside of the world looking in. They still had the ability to speak to one another telepathically. Pegasus was plotting their escape just as he had done numerous times unable to break the force field that surrounded them. He tried his magic horn nothing. The phoenix also tried to break her confines to no avail it was too strong. Pegasus we cannot go on like this to be enslaved in some book forever that is not life what can we do. I know what you are saying but Merlin is a powerful enemy he has skills beyond my comprehension It is a damnable mess we are in now brothers and sisters we will have to bide our time for now. Merlin called to Uther as he was riding back to Avalon.

Uther the time has come I need you to return to Avalon and make ready for our arrival. Solana and Gawain on their way back as well. Tarnish and myself will be their soon. Yes Merlin I will await your return. Uther mounted his horse headed back to Avalon. Tarnish and Merlin were about two days ride to Avalon Merlin suggested that Tarnish ride on without him. Tarnish questioned merlin suggestion, Are you sure Merlin? It could be dangerous to split up right now. Merlin was grateful that Tarnish worried about him so Tarnish I for see no problems do not worry I will not be far behind I must gather the final materials for the staff of power. Tarnish was reluctant to leave Merlin on his own as he hesitantly agreed. Merlin I wish you good journey The same to you my friend Tarnish followed the path back to Avalon as Merlin began to stray back to the his sanctuary Merlin was just out Salisbury Plain. Merlin lifted the force field to enter the massive stone hinge circle on the center of the colossal structure stood large rounded sphere. Merlin looked at the marvel with such admiration. He reached out his hand and pressed against the round ball of silver. The sphere shifted as a semicircle opened. Merlin entered the sphere. Once inside he grabbed the emerald necklace of the vampires as well as the ruby dagger Merlin closed the ball as he exited his sanctuary he concealed its presents again. Merlin mounted his horse with all the materials for the staff of power so at last he could create the book of beasts bringing back the balance of the world.

Desmoria escaped the clutches of her imprisonment to find all the druids dead bodies chained to the wall headless. Desmoria thought she would have to face the same dreadful fate to be doomed to Hellfire for all eternity. Desmoria started to think back to before the attack. Yes of course. She remembered that her one of the most promising druids Dorothya had gone missing. I must find her she is the only one who can help me now. Desmoria left the castle in search of Dorthya.

She knew that she needed to find Dorthya quickly Desmoria would use a locator spell to find Dorthya.   When all the druids enter the castle, Desmoria marked them with magical brand.

She returned to the bowels of the castle were the lifeless bodies of the druids hung. Desmoria collected some of the druid's blood into a small goblet. She took her finger as she stirred the cold black blood of the druids.  She drank of the druid's blood chanting the spell to locate Dorthya. Desmoria close her ruby red eyes as she concentrated on Dorthya face watching as images swept through her mind forests and woods deep in the lush green landscape. She is in the gotlum forests.  Desmoria raced to the courtyard to the stables as she saddled her horse to ride into the woods. She entered the forest Desmoria reached for her amulet to hone in on Dorthya . The deep purple was glowing vibrant the closer Desmoria came to Dorthya .

Dorthya was roaming the splendor of the forest enjoying nature s she heard Desmoria walking toward her. She knew that Desmoria would find her as there was no need to run.

Dorthya called out" I am here Ezerbeth." "Come out Dorthya do not make me chase you, come to me know driud."

"I am coming my lady do not grow angry. I left out of fear my lady I would never betray you." The small meek woman walk out slowly toward Ezerbeth I have no time for lies or your insolence now come here Yes my lady what has you so distressed Again I have no time for your deceit you know what happened do not pretend but it is irrelevant now. I must summon Cronos I must return to my time. Dorthya was taken aback of what Desmrioa/Ezerbeth was saying "you mean you are not the queen. Who are you then?"

Desmoria interjected, "I have no time for this you must help me to summon Cronos enough of your chatter." Dorthya replied, "Yes my lady what would you have me do?"
Desmoria instructed, "We must build an altar of time in order to summon the Father of time. Yes my lady what do we need to build such an altar? You must gather you must gather the oldest wood in the forest. I must call upon the powers of time I need an hour glass and a sundial. You must hurry quickly gather the items I request and come back here without fail Dorthya. "Yes My lady I will do as instructed."

Desmoria already lost Dorthya when she ran away she would not take that chance again  Oh by the way Desmoria reached out and grabbed Dorthya by arm as she racked her sharpen claws against Dorthya arm. Dorthya knew instantly that Desmoria had poisoned her blood to keep her from abandoning her once again. I will cure you when you have finished the task Dorthya and only then now off with hurry. "Yes my lady" Dorthya replied. Dorthya ran into the forest her arms burned every step further she moved away from Desmoria the pain grew more intense.

The druid called out to the trees trying to find the oldest tree on the edge of the forest stood an old elm that has stood since the dawn of time towering above the rest of the trees look dwarf compared to this elm the lovely bouquet of soft lush green leaves the array of branches that weaved throughout it was magnificent.

 The trunk was gigantic, the roots of this tree stretched for miles. This is the oldest tree in the forest Dorthya proclaimed, Dothya stood in front of this mammoth tree she began to sway back and forth in front of the tree. Dorthya began to chant,

"By heaven light, power come within the night let this force come to the ground, May this force be never bound. From the North to South from the East to West. She focused all of her power into Elm tree as she picked up its dead leaves as she continued to recite:

"I conjure thee, I conjure thee a magical seed Dorthya took a seed from her cloak and planted it in the ground. As I plant this seed in the ground. May all force of magic gather around. For this I rekindle my magic flame, with this force may nature never be the same, I stand here tonight to gather what was lost, For without this gift my world will turn for the tossed, Bring to me what is mine, Let it come within the hour of time."

The tree started to become uprooted as it began to float into the air each branches began to separate the lush green leaves falling to the Earth as the bark from the Elm also fell leaving only fresh logs as they levitated throughout the forest to where Ezerbeth/Desmoria waited the flying logs started to descend right in front of Ezerbeth/Desmoria feet. One by one the logs fell into place creating the altar. The altar was a rectangular shape made Elm wood. Atop the altar was a large fixed piece of Elm. Dorthya ventured into the village to find the sundial and the hourglass at the local bazaar. She found both items and headed back to Ezerbeth/Desmoria, "Hurry come quick do you have the other items?"

"Yes my lady I have the hourglass and the sundial. Good now break the hourglass across the altar spread the sands of time all over the altar. Ezerbeth/Desmoria took the sundial in hand as she called to the god of time Cronos. "Hear my call Cronos send me back to my time Send me back to Merlin and my destiny," The sand atop the altar started to take shape of a man , "Who calls upon Cronos" this figure asked. "It is I Desmoria that has called upon you Cronos" Desmoria bowed to Cronos "I beg you god of time please aid me in my quest, I need to go back in time I need to stop Merlin before he becomes all powerful. Please Cronos can

you help me." "Yes I will aid you once more Desmoria," the figure blew sand off his hand as a portal opened. "Here is the doorway to the past you seek walk through it," Desmoria. Ezerbeth/Desmoria stood looking at the portal she must end her possession Desmoria grabbed her amulet as she chanting the spell of downfall. "Here me gods I cast out this form I call upon the magi of my forefathers to rid me of this bond "I Desmoria am ready to take control purge me of this wretched soul."
As she chanted her body started to quiver and shake her chanting become louder as her eyes rolled inside her head. She fell to the ground convulsing Desmoria started to change. Dorthya watched in fear at the transformation before her eyes Dorthya was overwhelmed as she simply replied Amazing. Desmoria surfaced a radiantly beautiful women as Ezerbeth body lay lifeless on the forest floor. Desmoria went through the portal hoping to get to Merlin before it was too late. Lucifer would have his just desserts when she turned Merlin to evil that is when she would unleash her vengeance on Lucifer. Desmoria walk throughout the time stream near the sage wood forest. The landscape was very different than she remembered it was devoid of life Desmoria scanned her surroundings. She heard a horses hooves approaching hard and fast. She looked to see lone knight riding Desmoria was quick to act she let out a loud blood curling scream Tarnish heard the terrifying scream above him in the forest the terrain was too rough to take a horse so he tie his horse as he dismounted and headed up to the forest on his guard he had his sword at the ready when he heard another loud scream this time. Tarnish ran towards the scream Desmoria hurried to a nearby fallen limb as she nestled herself under the limb to look like she was in distress,

Tarnish rushing to her aid of the helpless women. Tarnish on closer examination saw it was Desmoria but before he could react their eyes locked as she placed him under her spell. Tarnish stood motionless. Desmoria arose from her trickery. She circled her prey smelling the aroma of his haste and fear as the adrenaline was coursing through his veins. She moved in close to sink her fang deep into his neck when she heard hunter approaching. Desmoria grabbed Tarnish lifting him into the air as they went back to her lair. She set Tarnish down as she was the one who liked to play with her food. Desmoria took her hand striking Tarnish with her sharpen nails as soon as her hand stuck Tarnishes magic armor shooting pains surged in her arm into her chest and down her spine. She hissed as her fangs protruded outward. Tarnish was still under her control. She made him strip off his armor. Tarnish took off his armor. This time she was not waiting it was time to go in for the kill. Desmoria went in for the kill just as she was about to bite Tarnish he become disenchanted. Tarnish struggled with Desmoria as she fought with him pushing him to the ground knocking him out Desmoria went in for the kill. She sank her fangs deep into his chest as she drank of his life force leaving him dead. She levitated in search of Merlin. Tarnish lay lifeless as his body started to quivering uncontrollably. Tarnish eyes started to flutter blinking rapidly as he awoke his mine was hazy as his senses started to heighten. Tarnish's eyes widen with rage as he realized that he had become what he truly hated as his fangs emerged from his mouth he hissed in effigy. Tarnish was a Vampire. Tarnish was hit with this huge hunger pain. He heard a wild stag in the distance like flash Tarnish bolted in the stag's direction in the blink of an eye Tarnish attacked the stag clutching the magnificent animals in his arms. He sank his fangs deep into the flesh of the stag drinking it's blood Tarnish was not satisfied with the stag's blood he was still so ravenous for more he feast on the animals flesh in all leaving nothing but bones in his wake.

# CHAPTER FOURTEEN
# THE STAFF OF POWER

Gawain and Solana were riding back to Avalon as instructed by Merlin. Uther was also on the road back to Avalon. Gawain had noticed that a one rider was just ahead of the Solana and himself. Gawain motioned to Solana to slow down her horse, "What is it Gawain?" questioned Solana. Slow your gate my lady there is lone rider ahead he is not wearing any colors I believe he could be a threat. I want you to stay here while I scout ahead to gauge if he is a friend or a foe."

Gawain slowed his horse to a canter trying to catch up with the lone rider Gawain yelled, "Rider you there I am King Gawain who are you?" The rider found it hilarious that is friend Gawain did not recognize him sniggering his replied, "You must know me surely you jest King Gawain it is I Uther Pendragon I am heading back to Avalon to meet up with Merlin just as you are." Gawain shout back, "Lady of the Lake it is Uther." the Lady of the Lake rode forward to catch up with the men who were reminiscing about their adventures.

Solana wanted to hurry back to Avalon as she interrupted the men, "We must hurry back to Avalon without any delay." The men agreed, "Let us continue." They all quickened their horses riding fast and hard hurrying to reach Avalon before nightfall. The sun was still vibrant in the sky as They all came upon the forest Tarnish emerged from a thicket of woods as the sun hit his skin started to burn he hissed with his fang protruding directly at Gawain, Uther and Solana Lady of the lake. Tarnish was gone in the blink of an eye back into the woods. Merlin gathered all the provisions to make the staff of power he was headed back to Avalon when he was overcome with a vision.

Merlin stood unmoved right outside his sanctuary as blurred images started to focus in his mind's eye Merlin witnessed as Desmoria arrived back thru the time stream. She was scanning her surroundings as she saw Tarnish in the distance. Desmoria tricked Tarnish into believing she was a damsel in distress luring him into the woods. Once he was in her sites and their eyes met he was placed under her spell.

Merlin watched in horror as Desmoria fought with Tarnish. He saw in the fight how Desmoria's blood mixed with Tarnish's then she over powered him as Desmoria fed upon him and left him for dead. It was all too real for him just like his sister Mab created another Desmoria did the same. Desmoria levitated to the skies little did she realize that Tarnish was not dead as she had thought.

Tarnish was now what he truly disliked he was a vampire. Merlin was mortified to see Tarnish make his first kill the savagery of it was truly barbaric. The vision faded as Merlin was overcome with rage. **So she has returned the vile bitch. Now she is attacking the rest of my family I must stop her. I must prevent this Tarnish will not face the same fate as my sister I can save him.** Merlin leapt into the air flying fast and furious as he reached the veil of Avalon. The mist of Avalon were magic it was the heart of the dragon's breath that make the mist of Avalon. Merlin knew that he must immerse the branch of the great oak in the mists of Avalon as he chanted the spell of purification Magi Power from within sanctify this staff with purity, magi power protect this staff from evil within me. Assist me in this task be done, banish this darkness with the power of the sun. Merlin took out the ruby daggers as he pricked his finger he ran his blood down the staff with this I purify that only one of true heart may bear

The staff of power open of magi blood I proclaim will wield this staff and bare my name. So it will be so it be done. Merlin held the staff of now embedded with his blood and the dragon's breath it is now purified and ready to receive the jewels of prism. Merlin knew he had to act quickly.

Merlin needed the aid of Vulcans. He was not a very well-known god because of his childhood. His mother Hera saw he was very ugly and lame. She threw him from Mount Olympus. He fell and landed into the ocean, where he was brought up by the Nereid Thetis and the Oceanid Eurynome. Because of this fall, he was crippled. He remained with them for nine years and worked as a blacksmith, making all kind of beautiful things.

When he grew up, he wanted revenge. That's why he made a magic gold throne that he sent as a gift to Hera. When she sat on it, she was magically tied by invisible chains and she couldn't go anywhere. The other gods begged Vulcans to come back to Olympus and free her, but he just declared he had no mother. Greek god Dionysus got him drunk and brought him to Mt. Olympus on the back of a mule. He finally freed Hera when he was promised the beautiful Aphrodite as a wife. Vulcans was the only god who could help Merlin make the jewel prism because of his knowledge of blacksmithing.

Vulcans was lame so he was always on his mule. Merlin had to build an altar made of silver on the altar he placed a large anvil with a huge hammer and tongs. He called to the great Vulcans Oh god of fire and metal who forges the gifts god gives to man I call upon thee Vulcans show thy self I offer you these tokens he hold up the anvil and the hammer as he strikes the anvil three time Vulcans show yourself. Merlin pick up the tongs as he opened and closes them three times Vulcans show yourself. Merlin stood next to the altar awaiting Vulcans as large streams of fire started to shoot out of all four sides of the square altar an explosion of lava Vulcans appeared.

He was a large man covered in soot with sweat upon his brows as he sat upon his mule with his crippled feet turned backwards his bread was covered in ash his hair was unruly about his weathered face was course with disfigurement. "Who has called upon me?" Merlin stood a mere insect to the large man as he spoke, "I summoned you great Vulcans I Merlin am in need of your help. I have gathered all the materials to build the staff of power great Vulcans. The Lady of the Lake now approached with the final piece of the jewel prism Will you aid me in making the staff of power Oh Great Vulcans?"

The Lady of the Lake, Gawain and Uther arrived just outside of Avalon. Solana lifted the veil between the world to see this colossal giant of a man covered in soot and ash with his weathered face scared and mutilated. Astride a mule as his crippled feet were curled and facing backwards.

Vulcans bellowed, "You have all the materials for the jewel prism as well as the staff? I will aid you Merlin in your task provide me with the materials." Vulcans wanted to make the staff and use it for his own devices for his wife Aphordite was unfaithful to him. She borne him a son that was not his it was her lovers. Vulcans knew if he had the staff of power he could inflict upon her a curse.

**Comment [BP]:**

Merlin could read his thoughts and knew of his plans. That is why he had purified the staff before summoning Vulcans. Merlin handed Vulcans the jewels of time first then the ruby daggers and lastly the emerald necklaces of the vampire Vulcans took the jewels in his mighty hands he began to forge the jewels together making a diamond of all colors. Vulcans made the jewels of prism. Merlin awaited for Vulcans to ask for the staff he was shrewd to wait for when Vulcans asked for the staff

Merlin retorted, "Did you really already make the jewel of prism let me see that it looks imperfect to me." Vulcans was one of great pride when it came to his work he sought after approval for all his projects so with hesitation he gave Merlin the jewel prism. Merlin held the prism in his hand as he chanted the purification spell upon it, "Magi Power from within sanctify this jewel prism with purity magi power protect this jewel prism from evil within me. Assist me in this task be done, banish this darkness with the power of the sun." Merlin took his finger that was bleeding once more he ran his blood down the jewel prism with this, "I purify that only one of true heart may bear the jewel prism. One of magi blood I proclaim will wield this jewel prism and bare my name. So it be will so it be done."

Merlin took the jewel prism as well as the staff and held them over his head calling upon the power of the elements. The staff was forever fused together never to be torn asunder. Vulcans was enraged by Merlin and his crafty plot as he replied, "Merlin you are a great clever one you have outsmarted me. I did want to use the staff of power to make my wife pay for her adultery."

"I bear no ill will towards you Vulcans. I do not want to quarrel over this I knew of your plan but I will give you this instead may it help in your revenge upon your wife." Merlin held up an enchanted web. The web was made of golden chains that was invisible to the eyes of the beholder the web was unbreakable even for gods. Merlin told Vulcans to let Aphrodite lay with Ares when they are in their tryst ensnare them in this web bring them to Mt. Olympus to face their fate before Zeus. Vulcans was grateful to Merlin for his help as he returned to Ocean Volcano.

Merlin headed through the courtyard into the great hall were The Lady of the Lake, Gawain and Uther stood dumbfounded. Merlin headed to the sanctuary where the dragon's skin lay. Merlin took the staff of power pointed it at the dragon's skin with his other hand he let three drops of blood fall into the skin Merlin chanted the charm of making as the staff of power began to glow the jewel prism started to turn counterclockwise as the light from each jewel touched the dragon's skin. The dragon's skin started to change shape forming a hard bound book. The pages were almost bone like as the edges were sharp to the touch. Inside the book lands began to form first there were lush green forests with charming meadows.

The land spaces formed on every page each more miraculous than the last huge mountain ranges with snow covered peaks large wilderness with waterfalls and streams of cold clear blue waters valleys that were plentiful with all kinds of flora. Merlin called to the animals of war one at a time first Pegasus, then the Phoenix, the mighty Manicore, and last the Leviathan. Each animal had its own page in the massive book. Merlin had at last reunited the animals of war so that they could live out their lives in harmony.

The animals of war were not a threat. Merlin must make it so no one person could possess this book to unleash havoc upon the world. Merlin took the book of beast down, neither regions of the catacomb of Avalon deep within the gates of no return he placed the book into a force field protecting it for safe keeping. Merlin headed up to the main hall where Uther, Solana, and Gawain all stood.

## CHAPTER FIFTEEN
## TARNISH IS A VAMPIRE

Solana was the first to speak, "I don't believe it cannot be there is no way for this to happen I must have been mistaken in what I saw that is the only way to explain it don't you agree Gawain." Gawain who was still puzzled in what had happen outside the woods. He knew it was Tarnish but something was wrong with him that was for sure. Gawain mind still in haze replied, "What yes I think he must have been bewitched in the woods by something there is no way for him to become a vampire right?" "We killed all the vampires in that skirmish at the castle not a one survived as I recall. Uther what say you?" Uther who was well versed in being bewitched knew that something else happened to Tarnish his red eyes staring at us those dagger like teeth Uther had only seen that one other time and that was with Mab, I hate to say this to both of you but you are wrong there was a surviving vampire it was Desmoria she was borne of Mab remember she could have turned Tarnish into a vampire." I am sorry but I believe Tarnish is a vampire." Gawain was horrified to hear Uther's words as he injected, No it cannot be Uther Desmoria disappeared after the death of Norrick. Solana chimed in "Yes we both saw her escape from Merlin's wrath by jumping into the time stream." Uther was dismayed at the reaction of Solana and Gawain as he countered, "Yes we did but you see Merlin has returned so in turn Desmoria must have returned as well." Gawain applaud retorted, "Why would she turn Tarnish, what is her agenda." Solana who understood what Uther was saying commented, "Don't you see she wants to hurt Merlin she wants to make him suffer by hurting his companions she strikes at Merlin's heart that is her true goal." Gawain she wants Merlin to become so enraged that he turns to the dark side of his magi blood like Mab did. It all makes sense now. Gawain was a stubborn person by nature he argued, "No I believe that Desmoria is not that clever I believe if she has returned she was looking for food and Tarnish was in the wrong place at the wrong time? I believe she attacked him and in the struggle she overcame Tarnish and feed upon him leaving him for the beast to pick apart her leftovers. But in her haste she had turned him and he awoke a vampire." "Exactly right Gawain that is how it happened exactly," Merlin replied. I had a vision only moments before I arrived at Avalon Tarnish is a Vampire there is no doubt about it. Now we need to take action before the next blood moon or Tarnish will be forever a vampire. Gawain and Uther I need the two of you to capture Tarnish quickly before he does uncertain damage to himself or to others. Bring him back to Avalon place him in the caves of darkness deep within the catacombs of Avalon. Imprison him there and wait for my return. Solana you most protect Avalon at all costs do not let Desmoria gained entry to try to release Tarnish out into the world. I will go in search of the Villous bitch Desmoria I will have my vengeance last for her killing off my family. Once I have killed her Tarnish will return to his mortal self once more. Gawain and Uther do you accept this quest what say you. Merlin we accept you saw him just outside Sagmiel woods ride there and hurry. The knights raced through the halls of Avalon and mounted there horses headed toward the Sagmiel woods. Solana I love you more than words can express I will face the vile enemy and vanquish this vampire once and for all from existence never 87to darken our world again. This quest maybe long Merlin embraced Solana in his arms as he drew her sweet face to his and held her chin to his lips caressed her with a passionate kiss. As he held her close to his heart "I will return my lady of the lake we will have our peace so that we can live out our days together harmoniously in everlasting love " "My precious Merlin, I will love you forever I hold you close to my heart always. I give myself to you so feed upon me and fill yourself with my essence so that you may be strong in this battle with Desmoria." Solana flung her hair back to expose her tender neck. Merlin bent down as he stroked her sweet flesh with his fingertips sent tingles down Solana's spine. Merlin's fangs sunk deep within her neck as she let him drink of her magi blood.

Merlin's gray eyes turned silver. Merlin fondle her breast suckling her neck ripening them Solana was wrought with anticipation her loin were on fire they ache for his touch. Merlin was growing more and more excited with every kiss caress her sweet flesh he took Solana in his arms as he carried her to the sanctuary. He laid her on the ground as he undressed her slowing removing her gown to reveal her tight body Merlin untied the ribbon as he gently removed it revealing her soft supple body. Merlin gazed at her ample breast so ripe for the picking. He lifted her skirts to feel her inner thighs as he moved towards her the hot glistening pool of love She in turn was aching for him as she slipped her hand down his leggings to feel his hard throbbing man flesh as she started to lick his hard member inserting it into her velvet mouth twisting her tongue around his manly girth Merlin thrust into her mouth slow and hard so he could feel her lips caress him. Merlin played with her teasing her loins fondling her body. Solana could not take it anymore she wanted him and she wanted him now. Solana jerked off Merlin's legging to reveal his erect hard flesh she begged him to enter her. Merlin took and placed her leg over his shoulder spreading her sweet luscious slit Merlin entered her. The intensity of arousal was apparent as she shouted. "Yes Ah that is it now" Merlin now as she grabbed ahold of his juicy backside trusting him further within her. "More yes more give it to me," Solana begged Merlin thrusted vigorously into the creamy white depths of Solana." Yes that it Merlin, "Yes "with explosions of ecstasy Merlin released. Solana was exhausted from their love making as she slumber Merlin arose ready to search for Desmoria to finally put an end to her terror. This was going to be a fight to the death he was going to seek his revenge for the loss of Norrick and Ursula. Merlin took the staff of power in his hands as he chanted a locator spell to find the vile bitch Desmoria The staff ignited as the jewel prism started to circle waves of light flashed in every direction north, east, south, and west finally the red beam of light pointed to the lands of the North to the kingdom of Glasgow Gawain Kingdom that is where I will find her. Merlin leapt in the air flying towards Glasgow in search of Desmoria. Uther and Gawain rode day and night searching the Sagimel woods for Tarnish but he was nowhere in sight. They had broken camp for the night and were starting a fire when they heard and eerie noise off in the distance. Uther spoke softly, "I will go Gawain you stay with the horses. Uther carries Excalibur at the ready as he investigated the noise. It was dark in the woods as an owl hooted Uther looked back for an instant as soon as he turned back Tarnish was upon him. His coursing red eyes he were covered in blood.  Uther unsheathed Excalibur as he did the emerald green glowing tint started to shine as a beacon of emerald light surrounded Tarnish he fell to his knees screaming in agony Uther shouted to Gawain "Come hurry Gawain I have found Tarnish." Gawain came rushing in to see his dear friend coward down under the light of Excalibur.  Uther motioned for Gawain to come closer with a hand gesture Gawain moved towards Uther as Tarnish lashed out trying to fight against the power of Excalibur.  He thrusted forward with rage as his fang protruded revealing the all-encompassing truth to Gawain there was no room for doubt now. Uther whispered to Gawain "you must subdue Tarnish so that we can get him back to Avalon. Gawain agreed as he headed toward his friend. Gawain was looking at a monster this was not his brother in arms anymore. Gawain balled up his mighty hand into a fist he struck Tarnish on the side of the face. As soon as his hand connected to Tarnish a shooting pain went corseting through Gawain as if he had stuck harden steel itself Gawain jumped as his mighty hand was throbbing. Tarnish laughed at the sure idiocy of Gawain. "I am a vampire Gawain you cannot harm me as I was mortal. I have evolved into a fierce creature of the night now." Gawain still enduring the pain in his hand retorted, "Tarnish it may be true that you are not mortal but none the less I see that even a vampire cannot with stand Excalibur as you coward there on your knees. Gawain lifted his immense boot off the ground as he jammed his enormous thigh into Tarnishes jaw sending Tarnishes head backward knocking him of balance. Gawain took his massive hand as he continued to hit on Tarnish eventually knocking him out. Gawain's hands were bloodied as he pickup Tarnish like a sack of potatoes he slung him over his shoulder as Uther accompanied him out of the wood,

It was nightfall now the sun had set and tarnish was headed back to Avalon a prisoner. Uther went to the saddle as he grabbed some harden leather to bind Tarnish for the ride. Gawain as distraught at what he had done to his longtime companion now turn enemy. Uther approached him understanding his great sorrow Uther gently placed his hand on Gawain's shoulder you had to do it Gawain it was the only way. Gawain looked to Uther with tear stained eyes, He was our brother Uther He was our friend now look at him if only we had been here if only we had prevented this horrible event. Gawain there was no way to foresee this It is not our fault this happened all we can do is try to fix it before it is too late Tarnish has yet to taste human flesh there is still time to save him from this fate now we must hurry back to Avalon before sun rise or he will be lost to us forever Tarnish is now creature of the night so mount your horse, Gawain wiped the tears from eyes as he mounted his horse with Tarnish on the back as he lay unconscious. The men rode most of the night as they approached the mist of Avalon. Uther called out Lady of the Lake Solana we have returned please part the veil so we may enter Avalon. Solana was sleeping heavily from her tryst with Merlin Uther beckoned again this time he shouted Lady of the lake We have returned please part the veil so we may enter Avalon and hurry. Solana awoke startled as she rushed down to greet Gawain and Uther it was still the dead of night. Solana emerged on the shores of Avalon as she lifted her arms to the god embracing the goddess as her half-moon started to glow as she closed her arms downward the veil between the worlds was open. Gawain and Uther dismounted quickly as they both grabbed Tarnish. Uther beckoned Solana to hurry they quickly went through the great hall to the main sanctuary as Solana open the catacombs so the men could take Tarnish to the cave to imprison him until Merlin return. Uther felt Tarnish beginning to awaken as his body started to shift Uther knew that the harden leather would not hold him long. Gawain hurry Tarnish is coming too Gawain picked up the pace as they went deep in to the catacombs of Avalon Solana lighting the way with her half-moon they finally reached the enormous cave mouth Gawain and Uther tossed Tarnish in as he was about to break free. Solana started to chant the minute his body entered the massive caves mouth Solana visualize the fire bathing her with glowing, protective light. The

fire creates a flaming, shimmering sphere around her as she chanted , "Craft the spell
In my fire Craft it well weave it higher weave it now of shining flame
none shall come to hurt or maim.
Fire within me now I cast none shall pass this fiery wall none shall pass
No, none at all." Fiery wall surrounded the caves mouth Tarnish on the other side was trapped imprisoned until Merlin's return. Uther Gawain and Solana left the catacombs

# CHAPTER SIXTEEN
# DESMORIA'S DOWNFALL

Merlin headed to Glasgow in search of Desmoria. Merlin flew fast and furious throughout the land all the while thinking, **Why would Desmoria choose Glasgow what was he missing?** Glasgow was Gawain's Kingdom after all and Gawain was on a quest for Tarnish who did he leave in his stead as king? Merlin completed this for a long while as he flew. **I remember Gawain had mentioned he has placed his brother in charge of his kingdom. Why would Desmoria want to go there?**

Meanwhile back at Avalon Solana and the others awaited Merlin return. Uther who was perplexed with Ingrien in his every thought his heart was broken knowing she was with Garlois now it was no use to think of her at all she made her decision. Gawain too was long for his homeland to see his Kingdom and his court weighted heavy on his mind.

Gawain wondered if his brother was taking good care of his lands while he was on this quest. Solana was worried about Merlin more than ever now because once again he has left her to go in search of Desmoria. Merlin is seeking not only his revenge for the death of Norrick but for his whole family and now Tarnish's life hang in the balance as well. Solana and the others were so engrossed in their own thoughts that none of them spoke for hours.
Uther stood up as he exclaimed, "I cannot take this anymore!!! Solana Gawain I am in love with queen Ingrien it has weighed on my mind since the day she married Garlois. She is the half that makes me whole I must go and find out the truth for my own sanity."

Gawain was stunned he had no idea that Uther was so tortured by a women. Gawain too spoke up, "I too long for my homeland Solana it has been far too long since I have seen my family and court I would like to venture to my kingdom." Solana understood the knights needed to find answers but she also knew that the quest was not over.

"I understand good knights that you both are weary and tired I too have a need to live in peace and forget this horrible mess but Merlin is out there right now trying to make this right we have a fortnight left until the blood moon is upon us I pray you stay with me here at Avalon until then now let us all retire from this long day perhaps with some rest we can start fresh in the morn with a better understanding about what is at stake."

The two men were hesitant but thought better of their own needs and agreed with Solana for now. They all retired to their quarters Solana was so worried about Merlin she could not sleep. She went to the sanctuary and prayed to the goddess for guidance once more. Solana knelt down in front of the altar as she prayed

"Oh goddess of the mother to the immortal let me be reborn as your child let your light absorb my own allow me to become your vessel once more" Solana raised her hands to the heavens "Oh goddess embrace me into your arms again I call upon you to open the door Oh goddess hear my prayers I cast aside all sin Bathe me in your moonlit glow Oh goddess I praise you in Mt Olympus by Zeus on high as above so below I am your vessel."

Solana awaited with her hands raised to the heavens to hear the goddess reply. An enormous thunderbolt came down from the heavens as it struck the altar the goddess appeared. Her white robes flowing with a golden overlay her long chestnut brown hair pulled back by her golden crown. The goddess had soft features her sun kissed skin.

The goddess eyes darted looking around at Avalon as she saw Solana on her knees. She reached her hand down as she lifted Solana's chin to look at her. Her beautiful dark eyes look deep within Solana, "Why have you summoned me Solana?" Solana was still ashamed of her action toward the goddess as she tried to look away as she spoke, "I am worried goddess Merlin is in search of Desmoria."

The goddess was enraged with Solana as she replied, "Why do you trouble me with such minuscule things Solana what Merlin does is trivial at best to me."

"No goddess the balance has started to shift can you not feel it there on Mt Olympus?" The goddess was bewildered at the thought, "What do you mean girl spit it out."
Solana on bated breath replied, "Desmoria and Merlin have travelled through time they have shifted the balance of Mt Olympus and Earth."

The goddess was taken aback for a moment with the realization, "Tis true that there is something amiss Avalon seems to falling apart at the seams. I sense evil with these walls. What have you done Solana? The goddess questioned.

Solana was hesitate to answer for she knew the goddess would be angry with her for allowing a vampire with in the walls of Avalon.

"I...... I have Tarnish imprisoned in the catacombs he has been turned into a vampire by Desmoria. Merlin is on his way right now to defeat Desmoria and end Tarnish's suffering before it is once again unleashed on the world. The goddess was growing frustrated with every word muttered by Solana

"YOU mean to tell me that you have risked my temple you desecrate this land all for a mortal that has now been turned into a devils spawn vampire, He is here now. How could you do this? How could you think that was a good idea?

Solana fell to her knees as she asked the goddess for mercy. "Please goddess try to understand it was the only way to safe Tarnish from this fate it was the only thing we could do."
 The goddess's eyes widen with fury at what Solana was saying. The goddess started to see the evil vampire Desmoria she had taken over Glasgow castle. Desmoria had infiltrated Gawain stronghold as she weaved her web of destruction. Desmoria lured Januirus to her once she found out who he was she went right to work turning him and placing him under her power. Desmoria became the mistress of the Glasgow. Merlin finally caught up with her. Merlin used the staff of power to encapsulate her in a protective force field as he levitated her out of the kingdom.

Desmoria still had her magi amulet she broke the fore field as she took a vile from her person the vile contained a love potion once it connected with Merlin he was head over heels in love with Desmoria. The images faded and the goddess shook her head.

"Solana I have had a vision of the future I have not time to quarrel with you about the present you must hurry to fortify Avalon Desmoria is coming to take over this world as well as Mt Olympus. There is no time to lose call upon Gawain and Uther to aid you take this vile it is a powerful potion that will aid in releasing Merlin from Desmoria clutches but you must have the staff of power and the magi amulet before you use it. Once you have both take this vile give it to Merlin to drink the spell will be broken. Solana you must take the staff of power point at Desmoria and repeat the charm of making three times it will not kill Desmoria but it will send her to the underworld forever never to return."

Solana heard the goddess she went right to work on fortifying Avalon Solana called to Uther and Gawain as soon as the goddess disappeared Uther was the first to awaken, "What is it Solana? Why do you roust us at this time in the morn? Gawain yawned as he too was startled awake. "Yes Lass what could be so important? We must hurry knights Desmoria has enslaved Merlin and is on her way here right now. We must fortify Avalon before she enters for the worlds are doomed if we do not act now.

*If you enjoyed this epic novel please become a fang buddy on our fangsite on Facebook at www.facebook.com/CAMELOTTRUESTORY*

*Here are some other titles from Author Joanne Padgett*

*Vampires of Camelot
Camelot's True Story Part I*

*Vampires of Camelot*
*Merlin's Revenge Part II*

*Stay tuned for the next edition in the epic novel series set for release January 2017*

*Vampires of Camelot*
*Uther's Acceptance Part IV*